DRAMA QUEEN

Suchitra Krishnamoorthi resides in Mumbai with her daughter Kaveri. When not busy with her creative pursuits or running her art and candle shop she loves to climb mountains, raft down rivers and cook fondue. She has also written two books for young adults, *The Summer of Cool* and *The Good News Reporter*.

DRAMA QUEEN

So bizarre it's gotta be true!

Suchitra Krishnamoorthi

hachette
INDIA

First published in 2013 by Hachette India
(Registered name: Hachette Book Publishing India Pvt. Ltd)
An Hachette UK company
www.hachetteindia.com

SRD

ISBN 978-93-5009-669-7

Hachette Book Publishing India Pvt. Ltd
4th/5th Floors, Corporate Centre,
Sector 44, Gurgaon 122003, India

Typeset in Adobe Garamoud pro 11.5/15
by InoSoft Systems Noida

Printed and bound in India by
Manipal Technologies Limited, Manipal

FSC
www.fsc.org
MIX
Paper from
responsible sources
FSC™ C104740

Drama Queen is a true work of pure fiction. Any resemblance to people places and events living or dead, from the past present or future is not just coincidental but a deliberately cunning attempt to grab eyeballs and propel the book into the bestseller list.

PART-I

Will You Marry Me?
(But No Sex, Please; I'm a Good Girl, I Am):
An Emotional Odyssey of Lust, Betrayal and Text-Message Terrorism...

1

For a girl who grew up like every other girl of my generation, *soo* believing in the 'and-they-lived-happily-ever-after' blah about Cinderella, Rapunzel, Sleeping Beauty and a hundred other fairy-tales, the notion that 'happily-ever-after' could be a de-facto myth propagated by popular literature and other fictitious, brainwash art-forms has been a reality impossible to swallow.

Yes, I'm still a firm believer; my faith resolute and unshakeable. I know the nay-sayers are a dime-a-dozen but *I'm* a diehard. Willing to stand alone, regardless of what anybody else says, thinks or does.

'Are you *crazy?* Why on *earth* would you want to get married again? These fairy stories aren't real. Ever given a thought to how someone with a name like "Grimm" could write "Happily-ever-after" stories? Grimm means *sad* by the way…' My friend Sangita was in full form – at her patronizing best.

I was tired of her Amazonian ways. 'Thanks. I know that. I'm a writer who has already published two books – by the way.'

'I know you've written two books already and I'm proud of you, by the way.'

Oh yeah? Then how come your expression is telling me another story, my friend?

'By the way, Suchitra – did you know the Grimm brothers

were called Jacob and Wilhem?' Sangita informed me, eyebrows arching disdainfully.

It was obvious she knew I had no knowledge of the history lesson she was about to impart. And, really, that was the only reason she was telling it to me at all – to show off her superiority: 'Wilhelm got married and Jacob never did. And Wilhelm basically wrote these stories to give his unhappily married brother Jacob hope that he too would be happy one day. Their stories have tricked us all into believing this "happy ending" fallacy for centuries. Did you know that?'

Uff! I *so* hate cynicism. Sangita's intellectual snobbery at being the 'brain' from school who went on to excel at IIM–C (Indian Institute of Management–Calcutta) had always got on my nerves. The worst part was that she was so militant in her views. Always out to flaunt her heavyweight knowledge and gargantuan earning skills. 'Look at the way you talk down to others, as if they are morons,' I was determined to give it right back.'Who the hell is interested in whether the Brothers Grimm got married or not? All I said is that *I* want to. Really, Sangita, can't you *ever* stop showing off?'

Sangita held her head up another notch.

'I *don't* talk down to others and I don't treat you like a moron even though most times you behave like one. You're the one suffering from an inferiority complex. I just thought you'd like to know, that's all!'

That arch of the eyebrow and the toss of the head again. *Uff!* Girlfriends can get on one's nerves sometimes. 'Because *what?* Jeez, don't you get enough applause at your office? Why do you need it from *me* too?'

Undeterred by my scorn, Sangita continued: 'There's no

need to be rude, Suchitra. You've had a problem with me ever since school because I am the brainy one who did the MBA you always aspired to…'

Me? Aspiring to do an MBA? Was she bonkers?

'If I looked like you I would have no choice *but* to do an MBA!'

Sangita's looks had always been a sore point with her; I had touched a nerve. Good. That was *exactly* my intention. *Gotcha, girlfriend!*

'Oh ya? And what glory have your glamorous looks and talent got you? Your failure and unhappiness is not anybody else's fault. Listen, Suchitra, I left a very important meeting and came here because I thought you were depressed…'

'I'm not a failure and I'm not depressed. I just said I want to get married because I'm tired of being alone. Being on your own is just too much work.'

'What work?' – Expression getting bitchier and bitchier by the minute.

'Looking after a child single-handedly is a *lot* of work. You can do what you do only because you don't have kids. Thank god, you don't have a husband. I mean, you'd probably expect him to breastfeed as well…'

Trying hard to hide her shock, Sangita said, 'Stop making excuses! Kaveri is grown up enough now. I suggest you start doing some real work. Find yourself a proper career instead of hiding behind the burden of single parenting and this pining for a man. What good has it done you?'

'Look – forget it. You'll *never* understand, because a woman like you doesn't need a man. You've turned into one yourself with all your aggro tendenceis. All that's missing now is a moustache!'

I *hate* confrontations but sometimes they are unavoidable. And this one was long overdue. I was done with being a pushover and intended to let everybody – especially the likes of Sangita – know. Showing off all the time about her super-successful career and foreign trips and new cars. *Nouveau riche* vern! She was definitely becoming a man. Even the way she walked and dressed had changed over the years. Now it was only pants and coats and boots. 'I work so hard'; 'I earn so much'; 'I'm the boss.' *Uff!*

'If looking after and taking responsibility for myself and my family makes me a man in your eyes, then god help you. The day I find the right person – and I hope that day's not far – I'll happily sit at home barefoot and bake cookies and enjoy the luxury of my blessed life instead of constantly complaining. And I suggest you move your butt and do some work too, instead of endlessly living in the hope that some man is going to come and save you. Believe you me, you have to save yourself…' Sangita ranted on, undeterred.

'I don't need anybody to save me. I want to marry for company. And love.'

'Love? Hah! There's no such thing. Look at you – you're a wreck!'

'Look at you, for god's sake. If I'm depressed – you're fat. You're pudgy *and* pompous. And yes – *ugly*!'

I had overdone it.

'Enough! You've gone crazy.' Sangita snatched up her bag and marched towards the door, her voice quivering with shock. 'I came over because you said you didn't want to be alone. But you've become so selfish and obnoxious it's hard to be around you…'

'I'm not selfish. And you're the one that's obnoxious – not me! '

Crash! Boom! Bang!

Sangita had left the building.

♋

Shrink said the problem was that I held in too much; held it in till it festered and erupted like an angry volcano, spewing lava. She advised me that it was better to let off steam a little at a time, on a regular basis, and to be true to myself rather than pussyfooting around others who tried to control me by attacking my vulnerabilities.

Now Shrink did have a name – Dr Something Something or *something* – but I no longer remembered it and she, rather pleased with the title, no longer reminded me of it. So I had asked, 'But, Shrink, if I'm going to say it, it will mean I'm revealing my feelings, *na?* Obviously, I'll say what I feel, *na?* How can I hide and reveal my true feelings at the same time? Are you telling me, Shrink, that I should become a liar and start saying exactly the opposite of what I'm *really* feeling?'

'No, of course not, that's not what I meant.'

'Then what should I do, Shrink? Conceal or reveal? Show or hide?'

My brain had started to curdle with confusion all over again. Dr Something Something and some other things seemed to be having that effect on me of late.

'Just be yourself, Suchitra. Don't worry so much. You'll be fine. We will discuss this in more detail in our next session.'

Phew! What a relief. Confusion sorted. Shrink was right.

So, big-time bridled at Sangita's bragging, that's exactly what I was doing today.

Being true to myself.

♋

'Did you *really* tell her that?'

I had dialled Chandni minutes after Sangita's dramatic exit; if not one girlfriend then the other. To hell with her, I had other friends.

'Tell whom what?' I chomped nonchalantly on some chocolate.

'Did you *really* tell Sangita that she has become very fat and ugly and that all she needs now is a moustache?' Chandni asked without preamble.

News sure spread fast in girlfriend land. In explicit detail, too. For all her corporate success and big-shot attitude Sangita was nothing but a cry-baby dressed up in a business suit. I would gift her bag of Pampers soon.

Chandni's sharp reaction was a bit surprising, though. Always affable and eager to help dog, man, and girlfriends, Chandni's defence of Sangita's superciliousness pissed me off further. Why couldn't she ask Sangita to tone down the gyaan instead of making all this sound like my fault?

'Well, she *has* become really fat and that is a fact…' I let the chocolate roll around my tongue and warm my throat, feeling another unexpected and deliciously irrepressible surge of courage: 'I mean, aren't girlfriends supposed to tell each other the truth?'

'Yes,' Chandni said, rather viciously for her, 'which is *precisely* why I'm telling you that *you* had better get a grip on yourself.

The truth is that you are becoming *really* rude, and losing it. *Completely.* Sangita only came over because you asked her to. Look, everybody has problems but…'

'What problems do you have, except what dress to wear to your kitty party, or how many times a week to have sex with your ooooh-so-loving husband?' I cut in angrily. 'Do you even have a count of how many servants you employ? Are you trying to make me jealous knowing fully well that…?'

'Why would I want to try and make you jealous? I am sharing my life with you, just as you share yours with us. Isn't that what girlfriends do?'

Lately, it had begun to seem to me that all my girlfriends were only flaunting their gloriously happy and fulfilled lives to rub in my own sorry state of affairs in my face. I didn't want to hear any more about their achievements or their money, or their sex lives. It was like someone in a car eating cake in front of a beggar and then spitting at him when he pressed his beseeching hands to the window.

'Stop it, Suchitra,' Shrink had scolded me when I had discussed my girlfriends' devious machinations with her a few days earlier. 'You're not a beggar and you're not begging. You are only asking god for a new life. Snap out of this negativity and assert yourself. No reason to hear them boast if you don't want to.'

Well, I definitely didn't. I was done. Who the hell needed a bunch of Cruela de Vils as girlfriends?

'You're not sharing, Chandni. You're showing off. Just because you know that I…'

Click! The line went dead.

I dialled some more numbers. Tanya, Preeti, Neeta, Kiran,

Anupama, Simran – they were all busy too. Or had they been tipped off about my abhorrent rudeness already? Why did girlfriends have to tell each other *everything*? Where was the need?

♋

With no one to talk to, I paced restlessly about the house; up and down and all around. *Phew!* It was the strain of being alone and my persistent insomnia that was making me so edgy. And the fact that Shrink confused me even more than my mother. Didn't they understand? Dang! As if the stress of trying to find a husband wasn't hard enough. Was I now supposed to find new girlfriends too?

I pottered about, my mind flitting from pondering such weighty imponderables like, if all nuts have shells why is a tortoise not a nut? To, why did y follow x? And, more inexplicably, why didn't my ex follow y? Aimlessly flipping switches on and off, staring at the peeling paint on the walls, I made a mental note of fading patches that needed touching up.

This was the one major pitfall of living in a city like Mumbai. No matter how much repair and refurbishment you undertook, your house was bound to start resembling a decrepit toilet if you didn't spruce it up every few months. *Uff!* I decided I would mark the blistered areas on the wall with a pencil as soon as I made myself a cup of calming, fresh herb tea from the little terranium I had planted on my kitchen windowsill.

I went into the kitchen and stared at my horticultural efforts. Most of the plants had withered and died of neglect, – but the mint still had a couple of leaves left. I should claim a refund from that terannium workshop that I had gone to – after all, hadn't they assured me that these plants would *never* die? Bloody frauds!

I banged about the kitchen trying to find a pair of scissors to cut the mint leaves from their stem. The glass jar of sparsely growing mint (surely on its deathbed; about to join the rest of my terranium in its grave) toppled over onto the grilled parapet behind the kitchen wall and broke with a loud thud. Dang! Was I supposed to turn into a gymnast now? Just so I could retrieve a few mint leaves to make myself some calming tea? Were my plants plotting against me too? Didn't god have *any* mercy left for me?

The sound of the smashing pot woke the maid, lying fast asleep on a chair besides the ironing table that held an enormous, neglected pile of washed clothes. She leapt up out of her slumber and stared at me with a mix of pretend concern and real guilt. It didn't for one moment mask her inherent laziness and cultivated vagueness:

'Madam, *aap ko kucch chaihiye*?' (Madam, can I get you something) she asked obsequiously. Avoiding eye contact, she immediately grabbed the first item of clothing that she could lay her hands on, furiously flattening out the shirt with a dead cold iron.

Uff! Who the hell was she fooling? I snatched the iron from her hands and touched my fingertips to it – cold as ice. Why was it that I seemed to invite only dumbos and dykes and lazy maids into my life? This one was a thief too. She had robbed me of my sleep ever since she had come to work for me almost a year ago. I would get rid of her soon. As soon as I...

Oh no? What was that noise?

Were Cupcake and Muffin fighting again?

Had Muffin contracted the 'red-stick' disease once more, in spite of me taking the precaution to neuter him after that first red-stick disease attack?

ꕥ

Cupcake and Muffin are my two cocker spaniels. Cupcake is the female spaniel I had gifted Kaveri on her birthday some years ago. Muffin, the male I brought home a few months later in an attempt to get Cupcake a love life. Because, regardless of what my girlfriends think, I am not a selfish creature after all. In spite of my lonely plight I understand that every girl needs a companion.

But it had been a big mistake.

Don't get me wrong. I *love* dogs. See, I've always had dogs for pets. *Female* dogs. Ever since I was a kid. But never a male dog. Because I find their appearance a bit…umm… *whatchmacallit*…unaesthetic.

Male dogs, in my opinion, should not be allowed to roam around without underwear.

My revulsion had started many years ago, when I was a kid no more than Kaveri's age and my neighbour's male dog – Caesar the Labrador – would barge into our home every time our front door was left open; a red stick attached diagonally to his underbelly. Panting and drooling and jumping and humping every object he came into contact with!

Of course, Caesar's attention was especially focused on my female Daschund, Bosky, who would tremble and whimper everytime he made an appearance. So in fear of my little Bosky being attacked by Caesar, I had taken to hiding her in the cupboard when he appeared and refused to be shooed away.

Unfazed by being denied Bosky's terrified, but unprotesting flesh, Caesar would continue to enthusiastically rub against cushion covers, stuffed toys and sometimes even my leg, the expression in his eyes manic and epileptic! *Eeks!* I had seen that expression in stray rabid dogs on the road and assumed they were diseased and mental. Encountering the same thing in your drawing room was another matter altogether. I remember feeling very afraid.

What exactly was Caesar the male Labrador doing? Surely there was something wrong with him, I had asked Amma, telling her of my attempt to detach the red stick from his belly that was obviously causing him some kind of discomfort and making him behave so weird that he was always trying to scratch the thing off his body.

Amma had said nothing to me, of course. But Caesar was forthwith banned from visiting our home with a stern warning to the neighbours to keep him leashed. 'That is a diseased dog. Sick. If he enters our house again I will call the police.'

I had spent many years believing that Caesar's red stick was indeed a great disease and was glad I hadn't met any other dog after that who was similarly afflicted.

Anyway, coming back to Cupcake and Muffin... On Muffin's first birthday Kaveri had thrown a small party for him. We'd ordered doggie cake, invited the neighbourhood dogs and sung happy woof-woof songs. It was also the day Cupcake got her second period. For a few days everything was smooth sailing. My pets were well behaved and we were one happy family. But one week later all hell had broken loose.

Muffin had suddenly started to go insane. Running aggressively behind Cupcake just like Caesar had run after

Bosky. Cupcake sometimes snarled to warn Muffin away or hid herself in corners where she knew he could not get to her. But Muffin jumped and yelped and scratched and banged at the door nonstop. He screamed and barked and whined all night long. Stopped eating; lost weight; moved around with eyes glazed. All his attention manically, single-mindedly, focused on getting to Cupcake – who continued to look bored and disinterested. My sweet little Muffin had turned into a psycho. Kaveri was frantic with worry – she wanted to know if Muffin had got the red-stick disease (now part of Krishnamoorthi family lore) and gone mental.

I had decided to keep Cupcake and Muffin in separate rooms till Cupcake's period was over. I even walked and fed them separately. Then one day I went out, instructing my maids to ensure that the dogs were kept apart, but within an hour Kaveri called me up crying loudly, terrified. 'Mamma, come home soon. Cupcake's and Muffin's bums are stuck together and I can't pull them apart. I'm very scared. I think Muffin has definitely got the red-stick disease.'

♋

This catastrophic, Nat-Geo scale, bum-sticking incident had occurred four years ago. I had since got both dogs sterilized. Things had calmed down considerably ever since and doggie peace was once again a given in our home. So what was going on now? Didn't I have enough worries on my plate without having a litter of spaniels to look after?

Trying to calm down and hoping that it wasn't indeed another attack of the red-stick disease (My vet had warned me that while neutering the dogs would ensure they didn't produce a litter it wasn't a definite guarantee against horniness) I asked the maid in my most clipped Memsaab voice, 'Why are the dogs making such a racket? Have you walked them for the night?'

'Yes, madam. But they did only sussu, not potty. Should I take them down again?'

'No need for that,' I snapped. I knew her tricks. Her boyfriend was no doubt waiting downstairs and the dogs' delayed potty would be an excuse for her *ha ha hee hee.*

'He's not my boyfriend, madam – he's my jijajee...'

'Jijajee? Brother-in-law? He's married to your sister? Does she know you hold hands and do *ha ha hee hee* with her husband who has conveniently got a job in the same building as you? Should I inform your sister of your treachery?'

'No, madam. Please don't do that.'

'Why shouldn't I? Considering you never complete your jobs because of the amount of time you spend doing *ha ha hee hee* with your jijajee?'

Now, what my maids did in their spare time after the chores were done, was none of my business. But when it left my home in a mess I was left with no choice but to push the pedal.

Especially today, with my freshly-made decision of refusing to be a walkover.

'Because he's not my jijajee, not *that* way, madam. But since everybody in the village calls him jijajee, I also call him that.'

Uff! Why did everybody mess with my brain so much? Why couldn't she just admit to having a boyfriend? What was the shame? *Wait a minute.* Had Chandni and Sangita been filling my maid's head with falsehoods, such as my likely jealousy of any woman who has a boyfriend or the hint of a sex life? Is that why my maid continued to lie to me in spite of the fact that...?

But then the dogs' barking got even more frantic. So I decided I would ponder her deceit as soon as I'd sorted the woofs.

'Please go check on the dogs and put them in separate rooms, I don't want any noise in the house. If I don't sleep again tonight I'll definitely die!' I said, sticking my nose in the refrigerator, looking for some more chocolate to calm my nerves.

The maid returned from the other room a few minutes later, eyes downcast, twirling her dupatta in her hand embarassedly. *'Mere se nahin hoga, madam. Meri shaadi nahi hui hai. Main nahin haath laga sakti...'* I can't do it, madam. I am unmarried. I cannot touch it...'

Cupcake and Muffin continued with their head-banging, hard-metal canine cacophony in the background. I winced... 'What do you mean you can't do it because you're not married? What nonsense is this? Didn't I tell you looking after the dogs is part of your job when I hired you?'

'Sorry, madam. *Mere se nahi hoga. Muhje sharam aati hai.*

Oh crap.

If the dogs didn't stop their barking and growling I would tie the dogs up in the car park for the night. Kaveri would be distraught if she found out and the Building Society would object but I would deal with that in the morning. It was driving me insane. Tomorrow I would call the maid agency and complain about this stupid girl's behaviour. Not for the first time, I resented the fact that my life was so entirely dependent on my maids and my staff. I couldn't even plan a weekend out on my own without begging a friend or family member to stay in for me and look after Kaveri in my absence. Her father, of course, had no such worries. He disappeared for months together, sometimes forgetting to call for days on end. Every time I suggested he look after Kaveri for a few days so I could give myself a little respite from momma matters, his business and importance quotient increased tenfold. So much so that contacting or accessing him was a more Herculean task than planning a coffee with the US President.

Really, I needed to be more assertive about that too. I couldn't take the unfairness of it any more. How can a father continue to enjoy the freedom of a bachelor when a mother's life falls apart from the pressures of parenting? I decided I would have a firm chat with Shekhar about that tomorrow itself. For now I needed to figure out why my dogs were going bonkers and had to stop them from driving me mental. I went to the room the racket was ensuing from.

Dear god! What *was* that in Cupcake's mouth that Muffin was so aggressively trying to grab? 'Cupcake! *Cupcake!* Come *here*! Show me what's in your mouth right now – naughty girl!' I yelled as I chased after Cupcake with Muffin following closely behind, the maid at our heels. After much huffing and panting, tumbling and grabbing I managed to snatch the object out of Cupcake's mouth.

Eeks – eeeeks eeks! Oh no! I flung the mortifying object across the room in horror. The battery within it turned itself on with the impact of the throw. It now vibrated and purred and throbbed, while Cupcake and Muffin barked even louder, dancing a little jig around it. It was the bloody dildo.

I would slap Chandni for this. In spite of my many holier-than-thou protests, this was the second dildo she had gifted me in the last few years. While I had got rid of the first by driving across the city in the dead of night and flinging it into a municipal garbage bin when no one else was looking, this one (gifted to me two months ago) I hadn't mustered the courage to dispose of yet.

Until tonight. Which is why I had wrapped it up in several sheets of newspaper, and many paper bags, and chucked it in the garbage bin. But how was I to know that three-day-old chicken wings had been thrown into the bin just a few minutes prior to the discarded dildo?

'*Madam, mein jaaon? Aapko kucch chahiye?*' 'Madam, can I go now? Do you need something?' The maid's eyes darted slyly between the chewed-up dildo and me.

'Why didn't you put the garbage out earlier?' I squawked, trying hard to keep the shame from my face, diving across the room with a pile of newspapers to wrap and cover the macerated, throbbing, plastic penis. I turned off the battery switch clumsily.

Muffin and Cupcake thinking it some sort of game continued to try and grab the dildo. The battery turned itself on again making Cupcake's cheeks tremble and wobble till she spat it out. The dogs boogied around the dildo, cocking their heads, barking and growling all at once. Oh god! Why would the floor not open up and swallow me. 'Go in and go to sleep,' I belched at the maid. 'And please finish the ironing first thing in the morning tomorrow.'

I decided there and then that I would gift-wrap the offensive object and send it to Chandni at her husband's office address. So he would finally know that the sweet, simple, homely housewife pretending to have nothing but Gucci and Prada on her mind was actually a sex maniac in disguise. I mean, how could a normal girl walk into a shop and buy a dildo? So what if it was in Amsterdam or for her friend?

Had she *no* shame?

♋

In spite of my repeated requests to her to shut up, Chandni had kept insisting, 'You need to have sex.' A diatribe she had persisted with for the last five years. Ever since my divorce. Setting me up on dates with losers, gifting me dildos and suggesting I watch porn, to stir life into my suppressed hormones!

'The way you live is not normal, Suchitra. Chocolate is *no* substitute for the real thing. I hope you at least masturbate?'

Really, couldn't this woman talk about anything else? Hell bent on dragging everybody into her sex pit. *Uff!*

'Don't be disgusting. I want marriage, not sex.'

'Oh ho, yaar – same difference. Why are you still so full of your Southie hang-ups? You have more hang-ups than the clothes in your wardrobe. Let's go shopping or something. Don't be depressed. You'll find a good man. In the meantime, all I'm saying is…You know that constant buzz you say you feel in your head? The static?'

'What about it?'

'It's just lack of sex.'

'I'm *not* full of Southie hang-ups. I'm *not* depressed and I *don't* want sex. And the buzz in my head is because I'm moving into the spiritual plane where the need for bodily and worldly desires ceases to exist. Understood?'

'Whatever, yaar. Listen, we have to manifest things for

ourselves. Think them and make them happen. Or you'll end up living life alone with your Ganesha statue and…'

'Oh yeah, you mean you actually *think* every time you buy yourself a 5 lakh Gucci bag? Have you ever earned a single penny for yourself, even once in your whole life? Aren't you ashamed of yourself, in a poor country like India, spending so much on trivialities? Only a brain-dead person would do that!'

If Chandni could rub salt in my wounds constantly, so could I. I'd squeeze some lime on top of the salt too, so it burnt real bad.

'If you're going to get nasty we'll talk later. Take care.'

As if it was so easy. How could I take care? And of what? My Ganesha statue?

Shrink says my obsession with Ganesha could be a closet phallic obsession, but really, I think that is too much. When I asked her to elaborate on her theory she said we'd do it in the next session, delicately reminding me of my outstanding bill. One of these days I'm going to get Shrink and Amma together. They would set each other right. And then I'd put Sangita and Chandni along with them with their Gucci bags and corporate suits and set the room ablaze. That would be my revenge.

Ganesha, a phallic symbol? Gosh! How could Shrink *say* that?! Imagine talking about god like that. That too my favourite god! Shrink also had the gall to tell me that if I *had* to pray, rather than go out into the world and make my life happen, maybe I should try a different god for a change. Like Laxmi or Durga or Saraswati. That would unleash the feminine side of me, which I had kept buried for no reason at all.

'When was the last time you…?'

'Don't talk shit about Ganesha, Shrink – he's my soul mate.'

'O-*kay. Hmm*... so if Ganesha is your soulmate, what is the kind of human you want to invite into our life as a husband?'

'Well, obviously, a nice guy.'

'What's your definition of a nice guy?'

'Someone who's nice. Kind. Takes care of me. See, I've lived a rather posh life – obviously I can't put up with any wannabe. So, yeah, rich.'

'Why do you think you are incapable of taking care of yourself?'

'Stop! I don't want to think. I want to marry! *Now!* And I want more babies before I menopause. What's wrong with that?'

'If babies are what you want, you can have one by yourself. Society has changed – you're a modern, independent woman. You don't need a husband to have a baby. You can do whatever you like; what is stopping you except yourself? Think about it.'

Think about it, and make it happen, my foot. If I had to manifest my own reality what about all those theories of karma, past-life, soulmate, cosmic timing, etc? I was too intelligent and had spent way too much time reading books on the occult to not know the difference.

But I excused Shrink her ignorance. You see, she too is Punjabi like Chandni.

2

Let's face it, the average Punjabi is more physically oriented and doesn't quite understand brain power and spirituality as much as South Indians do. They just don't have that depth. At least, that's what Amma always said. And though Amma always made it sound like being Punjabi was a great birth defect, or a crime even, I always stood my ground and tried to explain to her that Punjabis are not bad – just very different from us.

For example, during my school exams, while we oiled our scalps for concentration and high marks, Chandni did it to enhance hair growth. While we toiled over $E=mc^2$, Chandni struggled with almond paste + milk = fair complexion. But the fact that Chandni would soon marry a suitable boy chosen by her parents and do nothing but continue the almond paste and milk routine and host karva chauth parties was a given. Chandni never questioned what she was asked to obey, and her life ran smooth as her own skin. With a loving husband who was a super provider, superman and super-stud. Add to that her silver cutlery, weekend homes and Jimmy Choos – her life had no boo-boos.

Amma never bought that 'Punjabis-are-not-bad – just-different' theory of mine and stuck vehemently to her biases and phobias. When I insisted on marrying Shekhar, she was actually more concerned about the shallowness of Punjabis than the alarming age difference between us, or even the fact that all film folk are rogues. It's only after my daughter Kaveri was born – half Punjabi – that Amma reluctantly conceded, out of great love for her granddaughter, of course, that Punjabis could have any kind of goodness potential at all. But not in their pure Punju form. She was adamant about that. They were acceptable only if they had the good fortune of having some Southie genes mixed in their bloodline – like Kaveri!

'Listen, Suchitra. If you still believe in all this Southie/Punju nonsense just because it's what your mom says, you need to grow up. And in a hurry. No wonder nothing is working out for you,' Shrink had once said.

'Your shrink said that! My god! That is *sooo* against shrink protocol. You can sue her, you know. It's her job to make things work out for you…' My girlies had been shocked when I'd told them.

Maybe, I would sue Shrink after all. Good idea. She was compounding my misery big time and insulting my god too. Would give me something concrete to do in the next few days other than staring moodily at my Ganesha idol, dreaming of procuring a husband, and putting up with bitchy friends.

Celine Dion's wail, *'All By Myself – Don't Wanna Be All By Myself'* blasted through the speakers, pinching and knotting up my already gnarled nerves. My girlfriends had warned me to delete the damn song from my iPod.

'Listen to what you want to invite into your life, *na*, instead of all this weepy stuff? Play some love songs – like how about that song – *Let's Talk About Sex, Baby, let's talk about you and me, let's talk about all the good things and the bad things…*'

'I don't want to talk any more. I want to get married. And for love and children. *Not* sex – understood?' What *was* their problem? Going on and on about sex! 'My iPod, *my* wish.'

All By Myself
Don't wanna be – All By Myysellfff!
Any Moooooorre!!

Uff! Stop it you bloody witch! Show some damn mercy. I clapped my hands over my ears. I should have erased the pathetic song instead of putting it on repeat but now it was too late. The batteries of my remote control had died eons ago. I was too tired to get out of bed to flip tracks. It was already 2 a.m.

Now that my girlfriends had decided to gang up and conspire against me and my big sister Sujata was away in America visiting her daughter and my middle sister Sunita put her phone on silent every night without fail, who could I call at this hour who wouldn't bang the phone down on me and try to understand my plight? I couldn't possibly call Shrink now that I had decided to sue her and all.

My male buddies were not an option any more either. Ever since they had, to my absolute and complete horror, revealed their amorous intentions toward me not so long ago. Like Ashok, who had arrived at my painting studio one night and grabbed me, holding me in a tight smother till I thought my diaphragm would pop out of my eyes.

'Why can't we be together?' he had hissed plaintively.

'Are you crazy, Ass? (Ashok's nickname, which he seemed hell-bent on living up to at that moment.) 'I've never thought of you like that – you are my friend, my buddy…'

'Why not? You don't have anyone else in your life. Give me a chance.'

'But I don't feel that way about you…'

Ashok had been my all-night chatting buddy on many occasions. A shoulder to cry on through the trauma of my failing marriage; the only male point of view in my otherwise 'festering-with-female-company-only' existence. But even so I had thought of Ashok as just another of the chicks, like a sister even (much to his horror this time), and was aghast that he had been thinking of me differently all along.

'So you were just biding your time till I got divorced and you could make your move on me, Frankenstein?'

Well, so now it was katti between us. Ashok didn't talk to me any more. Tough. No 2 a.m. batti from my side either – what if he were to grab me again?

Then there was this other buddy of mine – Bhola – who turned out to be a maha-shaana midnight stalker. All I wanted to do was talk but he went all 'I love you; I want you now! Open the door or I'll break it down!'

Not that I feared any form of aggression from Bhola. He's always been a complete sweetie, living up to his name which means naïve or innocent. But weighing in at a 130 kilos, all Bhola had to do to break open my door was lean against it.

OMG! 'Watchman – don't allow anybody up to my flat without intercom-ming me first, okay? Even if you think they are my friends and have seen them here many times before.'

Two rotten apples had sullied my entire basket of male friends. Now I even smiled at them warily – what if they thought it a turn-on and piled on me? What did they expect me to do – fake chemistry? No, no, no – too boring. Even more so than the miracle of jojoba oil or how many times and in what position. It's what had compelled me to create the 'A' list on my phone.

THE AVOID LIST:
(It was long.)

- Avoid like the plague – midnight maha-shaana stalker Bhola.
- Avoid when in studio – Ass the new Frankenstein in my life.
- Avoid 1, Avoid 2, Avoid 3. 4, 5 etc., for the classified social-circuit Lotharios, random coke-heads and pile-ons.
- Totally avoidable – Life insurance and credit card agents and sales representatives.
- And finally AVOID – in all capitals – the guy I gave my number to at the nightclub in the dark thinking he's cute. We had even talked quasi-marriage and all that blah over the cacophony of head-banging retro beats. Till said potential mate dropped me to my car and I got a good look at his face in the streetlight. And recoiled in fright! Tequila had almost made me propose to Dracula! Avoid, avoid, avoid. Next time I'd stick to wine and I'd be fine.

I squinted long and hard at my avoid list and ruminated adding Chandni, Sangita and few of my other girl pals to it. Should I? Shouldn't I? But then the only people left to not avoid would be the school mums and the local grocers and… since I had run out of chocolate for company too, I started to get a bit paranoid!

All By Myself

Don't wanna be – All By Myysellfff!

Any Moooooorre!!

Aiyyo!

Uff! Stop! Stop it!

Why was sleep being so evasive tonight – as it had every other night for the past so many nights?

Finally, in light of my lonely plight, and because I had distanced all my other regular late-night comforters, I had no option but to call Nana, my father. I dialled my parents' home in Bangalore. It was cruel to wake them up at this unearthly hour I know, but then it was cruel of them to have brought me unasked into this hostile alien world. Why should I be the only one to suffer?

It was my chance to punish Amma too. Considering her constant rants about my duties as a mother – wasn't it high time I reminded her of her own?

The phone rang steadily without being answered. Why wasn't anyone picking up the phone? Had my friends told my parents about my recent bout of rudeness and tried to poison their minds against me, like they had done amongst themselves? To hell with my girlfriends! Once I got myself a husband I would definitely work on my plan of putting them all in a room together and setting it ablaze. While me and my sparkling, brand-new husband stood outside the room and laughed, watching them susser. I would let them out just in time, of course, so they didn't die or get charred. Can't afford to be a murderess; just need to scare them a bit, so that they stopped messing with my brain so much.

I started to slip back into my 'All By Myself' despondency. Calm down, Suchitra – inhale exhale. Breathe in breathe out. Now purse your lips together as if you're trying to whistle and breathe in and breathe out again and again. Inhale exhale. Inhale exhale. Inhale exhale. Inhale exhale. Why wasn't Nana picking up the phone? Pick up, pick up, pick up! *Pleeeaase,* Nana.

See, I'm trying to manifest my own thoughts but god is on holiday and nobody cares about me.

Not even my own parents.

♋

Amma's groggy voice, when she did finally pick up the phone after the 261st ring, sounded like a ghostly echo from a million miles away. Oh no! I wanted to speak to my dad not my mother.

'*Aiyyo*, Chittu, what happened, ra kanna? It's 2 a.m. Is Kaveri okay?' (Chitty is my pet name, which is always, and variously, being modified into Chittu, Chotu, Chittappa, Chittachi, Chintu – and whatnot and all that. Kanna is darling, angel, baby – and whatnot and all that.)

So typical of Amma to enquire about her granddaughter rather than me, I thought. I shouldn't have bothered to call.

'Chittappa? Sorry, I left the phone in the other room so did not hear it ring. Is everything okay? Why are you calling so late? And why are you crying?' Amma asked again.

'I'm not crying and everything is not all right.'

'*Aiyyo* – what happened? What happened, ra kanna?'

Now Amma's wails were louder than Celine Dion's as she called out to my father. 'Naanaaaa, Nanaaa. *Naanaaa!*'

Music and mothers are meant to calm people and quieten them – not rupture their eardrums and render them unconscious with their caterwaul. Tomorrow, when I got out of bed, I would email Celine Dion's website and explain this to her. Or maybe sue her too, along with my shrink for promoting misery and suicidal thoughts in those in pious and proper search of a husband. Just because *she* wanted to be all by herself, how dare she assume the rest of the world ought to be fellow sufferers? Witch! I would call my lawyer tomorrow for sure. Take out a litigation against Shrink, Celine Dion and…

'*Nana! Aiyyo, Aiyyo,* come soon. I think something has happened. Chittu is crying…'

'I'm not crying, Amma. I'm fine, just fine (then why was my speech slurring?) Fatigue. That's all. Just fatigue. And insomnia. Tomorrow I have to wake up at 6 a.m again, like on every weekday, to get Kaveri ready for school. Yawn. And then at 10 I have to call my lawyer. How can such a chronically sleep-deprived brain concentrate?'

'Are you sure? Then why do you sound like you're crying or at a funeral?'

'I'm not crying, Amma. That is the voice of Celine Dion.' Just talking was making me feel better. I started to giggle: 'I'm going to sue her tomorrow.'

'What is Celine Dion? Are you drunk?'

'I'm not drunk, Ma. Haven't slept for many nights, that's all.'

'Are you on drugs now, then? That was the only bad habit left for you to pick up. Is Celine Dion the name of some new drug in the party circuit? I know about all these rave parties and all that and what you were up to in Goa last year. Don't try to hide things from me.'

'If I was trying to hide things from you why would I call you at 2 a.m., Amma? Can you try and *listen* to me for a change?'

'I will listen provided you're not trying to hide things from me. Remember, I'm your mother.'

Amma's always been a bit hysterical – but this was too much. It's no wonder that I've turned out like that too. Paranoid and rude and hysterical and confused. Mostly confused.

I always knew I would have to work hard to not pass on this confused, hysterical, rude, paranoid gene to my daughter. After all, one's thoughts and behaviour are known to even alter one's DNA. I tried to concentrate on what Amma was saying. What was she going on about? Rave parties? Goa? A drug called Celine Dion?

I laughed. Amma's bizarre worries were ROTFL funny. If she was on Blackberry I would have sent her that one.

'*Aiyyo*, first you were crying – now you're laughing. Nanaa! *Nanaaa!* Come soon. I think Chitty is on drugs; she's behaving very strangely. Chitty, you better tell me what this Celine Dion is, there must be some treatment. I'll talk to Sudhakar about it immediately.'

Sudhakar is my big brother, the oldest of us four siblings. The brilliant doctor in the family, whose model footsteps I was always supposed to follow, being from the same brainy South Indian family and all. But my foray into television and modelling at the age of fifteen had dashed all hopes of a stellar academic career to the ground and shamed the family forever. Marriage to a film director had been the icing on this massive, umbrella-shaped cake of shame. A delicacy Amma had baked – *All* By Herself.

'These film fellows are rogues. Scoundrels! You will ruin your life,' Amma's words when I had been all of nineteen once again rang in my ears.

'I'll ruin my life if I continue to live with a family that doesn't understand their daughter. I *don't* want to do an MBA – why can't you understand that?' I had shouted back.

'Right now it's okay – you're very young, so wrong things happen, but it's not too late to rectify your mistakes. Why don't you at least meet Venkatesh – he's a brilliant chap. Heads the institute of brain sciences at York University...'

'I love Shekhar.'

'Love Shekhar, aa? *Aiyyo*, you are too young, ra kanna. It's just an infatuation.'

'No, it's not! How can you understand anything about love? If you did you wouldn't keep yelling at Nana and us all the time.'

'Naanaa. *Naanaa!* Come soon! Chitty is talking very strangely about some drug called Celine or something,' Amma's voice snapped me out of my not-so-fond reverie.

'Don't be silly, Amma. Celine Dion is not a drug, for god's sake. She is one of the world's most famous singers. Remember I used to sing her songs in school?'

'Have you phoned me at 2 in the morning to remind me of what songs you used to sing in school? What is *wrong* with you? Do you care about your poor old mother at all? Have you enquired about my knee or my health in the last one week? Selfish! Do you think I have nothing better to do in life than listen to what songs you used to sing in your schooldays? *Naanaa – Aiyyo*, where *is* that man? He has gone deaf – never hears anything I'm saying.'

I shouldn't have disturbed them. I felt bad. 'Don't wake up Nana now, please. It's all right. Kaveri is fine. I'll call tomorrow.'

'I wish I had gone deaf instead of him – at least then I would not have to listen to his snores all night long. Anyway why *have* you called? You better tell me now that I'm wide awake and can't go back to sleep with your father snoring like a buffalo. Imagine, he has the guts to tell me *I* snore.'

'Amma, you *do* snore. So loudly – I've seen the blanket over your face levitate.'

'Shut up. You better not let Kaveri see you doing all these drugs, Celine Dion, or whatever rubbish names they give hallucinogens these days. You're not even that young any more to be so irresponsible… and remember, *you're a mother*!'

'Amma, once and for all, Celine Dion is not a drug. I don't take drugs, I'm not drunk and I fully understand my responsibilities as a mother.'

'But you're still smoking, no? Don't you realize how it will harm your poor child? And don't you know it will spoil your voice? That is god's gift from your grandmother. If you're so cheap to smoke even now, why are you telling me about the songs you used to sing in school all of a sudden? As if you ever invited me for any of your competitions…you only ever called your daddy…'

'Amma, I didn't call you up to tell you what songs I sang in school. I phoned to tell you that I'm tired of being alone and I want to get…'

'You're not alone. You have Kaveri. She's okay, no?'

'Ya, she's fine. Gone to her dad's for the weekend.'

'Then why didn't you also go if you're so bored and sad that you have to wake up your poor mother in the middle of the night?

Uff! I really wish Nana had picked up the phone instead of her. 'How can I go there, Amma? She's gone to spend time with her dad.'

'So what? You're her mother. Why can't you also go there? Are you trying to say that a mother cannot go to her children's house?'

'Please, Ma. Stop it. You're always taking off at a tangent. I want to tell you something important.'

'What can be more important than a mother's concern for her child?'

'Can you please *listen* to me for a change? I want to get married.'

'Married, aa? *Aiyyo*! Why? What about Kaveri?'

'Yeah, I want to get married. And this is not about Kaveri. It's about me.'

'Then why didn't you go with Kaveri to her daddy's house if you're so bored and lonely? You better talk to your daddy or go to Kaveri. *Naanaa!...Aiyyo*! The day he hears me I can die in peace!'

'Amma, please don't wake Nana up. And I can't go with Kaveri to her daddy's house – we are divorced.'

'Are you trying to imply that Kaveri's daddy's house is not her house? Then whose house is it?'

'Of course it is her house.'

'Then why can't a mother go to her daughter's house? If you are trying to hint that *I* cannot go to my daughter's house let me assure you I have no such intentions anyway. I would rather live in an old-age home than put up with your bad behaviour and rudeness.'

'I am not rude to you. All I tell you is don't shout at the servants.'

'I don't shout at the servants. All I tell them is not to eat all the cheese and chocolate that I buy for Kaveri – what is wrong with that?'

'*Aiyyo*, let's forget all that, Amma. Listen. Just listen. You remember Iqbal from my college?'

'Iqbal, aa? That Muslim chap who looked like a goat?'

'He didn't look like a goat. He just had a long face, like Vinod Khanna. You always find all my friends ugly.'

'I never found all your friends ugly. I used to always tell you that Tanaya girl was very pretty – like Elizabeth Taylor. Have you phoned me so late to try and convince me that Vinod Khanna is handsome? I don't agree with you. Definitely not. That Iqbal fellow definitely looked like a goat and not like Vinod Khanna.'

'Iqbal doesn't look like a goat now and even if he does I don't care.'

'Then why are you suddenly talking about him in the middle of the night?'

'Because he got in touch with me on Facebook after so many years – he's also single and looking to get married. So I thought…I thought I also want to get married again and…'

'*Iqbal?* Have you gone completely mad? He's a Muslim and you're a pure vegetarian. Have you started eating *mutton* now?'

'No, Amma – not even egg. And what's the problem? Even Shekhar was non-vegetarian. Kaveri eats meat and chicken – you didn't seem to mind that.'

'So what? Punjabis are different – they don't expect you to slaughter a goat in the house. When Shekhar ate meat you bought it from a shop. Besides, Muslims will expect you to change your name to Shakira or Noorjehan or some such.'

'No, Ma, don't be silly. He's a modern doctor from…'

'Stop this rubbish. If you want to get married again you better remarry Shekhar. That is your best bet. He'll always take care of you and Kaveri…'

'Amma, Shekhar and I are divorced and…'

'I warned you not to marry him, that too so young. The age difference was too much but you were adamant and ruined your life. If you had concentrated on your career, or married Venkatesh…'

'I'm in touch with Venkatesh. He's on Facebook too, and single. And he weighs a 150 kilos and looks like a bald porcupine.'

'How can a porcupine be bald? I'm a teacher, ra kanna, at least get your figures of speech right. And looks are not everything even though I know you married Shekhar only for his looks and money.'

Uff! Amma was exasperating. Her reality of events and corresponding emotions shifted from moment to moment, as if she had absolutely no memory of the truth or the past; every utterance a cryptic brainteaser test, which one was bound to fail. No wonder, I was perpetually confused. It's why I had started keeping a diary all those years ago, even sticking photographs into them and all that. So, if Amma denied, refuted or made up something I had the evidence to prove my case.

Like, the time after we had returned from our Goa trip, when I was all of seventeen and Amma was livid that I had not emptied out my suitcase even three days later. 'If you can't follow the rules of the house you better get out. This is not some public hostel,' she had raged at me. It was the 21st time she had asked me to get out of the house. And I had had enough. Why have children if all you're asking them to do is leave? So I bided my time. I would turn eighteen in a few months. Modelling earned me enough – I was already contracted to do a music album. Film offers were coming in too. I felt sure

I could support myself and so I took up a PG, a paying guest accommodation.

'*Aiyyo,* why are you doing this, ra kanna? Acting is for prostitutes. You're a good girl from a good family – you will not be able to adjust to the big bad world.'

'Acting is not a profession for prostitutes! I haven't done anything to be ashamed of. I have two very good film offers already and I haven't done anything wrong to get them. They have fallen into my lap and I intend to do them. One is in Malayalam, opposite Jayaram, a superstar down South, and the Hindi one is opposite Shahrukh Khan. He's being touted as the next superstar in Bollywood.'

Amma had no interest or knowledge of films or superstars. Even as kids, movie watching was banned for us. The only exception being the Shabana Azmi or Smita Patil art-house, feminist cinema. The only fare Amma considered 'decent' and so worth a view.

'Who are all these people – Jayaram and Shahrukh Khan and all? Actors? Are you on drugs, Chittappa? Please come back home. I won't force you to do anything. If you want to leave your clothes lying about for a month or even a year, that's fine. I promise I won't even enter your room.'

'Listen to what I'm saying, Amma. *Please.* In the Hindi film I play a Christian girl called Anna – it's a great role. A dream debut for any actress.'

'You know why they make girls Christian in the movies, ra kanna? So that they wear short skirts and expose their legs and breasts. You're not like that. Please come back home.'

'I don't want to come back home. I know your tricks. As soon as I come back home you'll be asking me to get out again.

I had already decided the tenth time you asked me to get out to do exactly that – I was just waiting to turn eighteen.'

I wouldn't make the same mistake that Sujata, my elder sister, had. Fed up of Amma's tyranny and being forced to do home science when she had the marks for medicine, she too had run away. Only she didn't have the financial muscle to hang in there. And then Ribero Uncle – Commissioner of Police, Nana's dear friend and batchmate – had found her waiting to board a bus at a bus-stop and hauled her back into the fold of her tormentors. 'Don't you know only prostitutes loiter at bus-stops?!'

For an eight-year-old to be eavesdropping on a conversation stating that her elder sister had been rescued from prostitution was unimaginable trauma; the fact that I continued to hear it over and over through my growing years, simply unforgivable.

It had taken me over half a decade before I could muster the courage to question my parents' bizarrely puerile conclusion – their contention that Sujata should be grateful for being saved from a life in prostitution by their timely intervention. And all this only because she had been caught waiting at a bus-stop. 'You're too young to understand, Chittu. Decent girls from decent families do *not* loiter alone at night at bus-stops. She has shamed us greatly.'

'She was not loitering. She was running away from you...'

This fact, of course, was something my parents, encased in their holier-than-thou bubble of ignorant righteousness, refused to even try to understand or acknowledge. I persisted: 'Who says it's a sign of prostitution?'

'I don't know, ra kanna. It's what they say.'

'Who the hell are "they?" The faceless, namelesss "they"

who impose their skewed, evil chicanery on blind, gullible folk like you, who are too scared to disregard or question whatever tripe they are fed? Would these same "they" have dared call my brother a prostitute if *he* had been caught loitering at a bus-stop? Aren't these the same "they" that say a woman cannot enter the kitchen when she is menstruating? Or that a woman should commit Sati at her husband's funeral? Or that a girl-child is bad luck?'

'Enough, Chittu. Go to your room and no dinner for you today!'

Sujata had agreed to an arranged marriage soon after the 'you-are-a-prostitute-because-you-ran-away-from-home-and-we-found-you-loitering-at-a-bus-stop' incident. That had been her escape. Agreeing meekly when Nana advertised in the papers to find her a match. '*Suitable match required for homely, domestically well-trained, Brahmin, home science graduate...*'

My middle sis, Sunita, had done the same a few years later – agreed to an arranged marriage as soon as she was old enough to run. And me, the youngest, the contrarian. Certainly not 'domestically well-trained' and refusing to have my name flashed in matrimonial columns of the *Hindu* and *Indian Express* for a well-placed, suitable, Brahmin groom. Threatening to destroy the familial fascism of the *highly* cultured, *sooooper* brainy, Krishnamoorthi clan!

Here I was – in love with an older man, a divorcee, and a Punjabi! Wanting to be an actress! The shame! *Chheh!*

I lived on my own for two-and-a-half years during which time Sujata made sure I never ran out of money, sending me whatever I needed from Muscat where she had set up home with her Chartered Accountant husband. Now *that* was a decent profession – Doctors, IRS (Indian Revenue Service) IFS (Indian Foreign Service), MBAs – *these* people had real jobs. Nana was Commissioner of Income Tax who taught IT law at Jamnalal Bajaj simultaneously. What the hell was an actress, but a whore? And what exactly did a film director do? *Aiyyo, Aiyyo*! All sleazy ogres.

'Well, Shekhar is a Chartered Accountant also by the way– that too from London.' That had silenced Amma a bit; he was not so despicable in her eyes any more.

Whilst on my own, I never once ran out of funds and could hold my head high and live in the manner I was accustomed to. Mainly because Sujata, my darling big sis, arrived with large suitcases full of clothes, shoes and accessories every time she visited, to dress her baby sister up. It used to bug Amma no end.

Nana said nothing. He's always been the strong silent type. Making me feel like I was the most special and precious creature ever been created by god. He never said this in front of Amma, though – why give her another reason to get pissed off? So instead of trying to persuade me to return, Nana had had a telephone line installed in my paying guest pad, (those were pre-mobile phone days) given me some money, and got me some nice furniture and knickknacks for my new abode. 'Whenever you're ready,' Nana had hugged me, eyes brimming with tears, 'please remember that we are waiting for you. And should you need anything, anytime, I am just a phone-call away. Don't hesitate.'

'*Aiyyo*, Nana. Why are you supporting this madness? She's definitely on drugs,' Amma had said, even way back then.

Yes, Amma has always suspected me of being on drugs even though I have never touched the stuff. Somehow, it was easier for her to blame the cause of my rebellious thinking on hallucinogens. The fact that it could be the stifling oppression of her dictatorship was something she never allowed to cross her mind. In her thin-gauge turtleneck collar, independence or nonconformism had to be smashed like a mosquito under a sledgehammer. Before it turned into a vampire and had a chance to suck the blood out of the hypocritical shroud of respectability that the Indian middle-class buried their snotty noses in. I refused to buy any of that.

'You're too intelligent to waste your life becoming an actress, ra kanna. You can do much better. Never mind that you missed your chance at doing medicine by choosing the commerce stream, but you still can do your Masters in Business Administration.'

'I'm not interested in an MBA – and I'm not going to give my Bcom finals, either. The timing is clashing with this other offer I have for a Hindi film. Nothing has been finalized yet but...'

'*Aiyyo*, Nana. Why don't you say something? Please ra, Chittappa. At least give your finals (it was the only time Amma held my hand, wept and pleaded.) How can you be a college drop-out?'

'I can – try me.'

'*Aiyyo*, please, chilaka. Okay, don't come back home yet. I'll send you food every day and get all your notes copied and help with your studies. But *please* – how can my daughter not even be a graduate? You are so intelligent....why are you wasting yourself? Have an affair with this Shekhar Kapur also, even though he's old enough to be your father. No problem. If you think you're in love get it out of your system. But please, at least complete your graduation. Then, when all this madness is over, you can marry Venkatesh and do your MBA. Even I did my PhD only after marriage. Venkatesh's family is broad-minded. They will allow you to pursue your interests.'

'I don't want to marry Venkatesh or do my MBA.'

'Don't you love your parents any more, ra kanna? How can you do this to us?'

And so she went. On and on. Emotional hijack had always been her weapon. My brain/body/soul reeled from its pointed arrows.

And yet, Amma won. I did give my finals – in the midst of all the mayhem in my life. I didn't even bother to go to collect my result or graduation certificate. Amma did all that, mortified by my low marks, but holding her tongue. 'At least now you're a graduate. One day you'll thank me.'

If you get high marks you're a good girl and I will love you. If you don't, you're a bad girl and I will not talk to you for five days.

If you obey me, I will love you.

If you don't, I will be angry and your punishment is that I will slap you across the face and not speak to you for one week. Not even when you beg me to wish you on your birthday. I will make your cake, of course, because I'm such a world-class cook who even managed to squeeze in a diploma from the catering college, bang in the middle of her three PhDs.

This cake you can share with your friends so they can all gush about what a great cook your mother is and what lovely cakes she makes. And, of course, I'll buy you a birthday dress to wear to school and sweets to distribute to your friends. But only the type of sweets that I believe won't give children cavities. What I do is correct. Not what you want only because all your friends have it. I will organize all this for your birthday because I am your mother, after all. But since you disobeyed me and ate the apple from the pooja platform, even though I had forbidden you, I will not talk to you for a week. Minimum! Don't you know that was an offering to god?

How can you be so disrespectful?

♋

In my growing up years, in the eighties, my life to those on the outside seemed posh. Enviable, even. We lived in a large, sea-facing, four-bedroom apartment on Napean Sea Road. While it was not a childhood of affluence, (Like Chandni's who arrived in a Mercedes Benz and spent school breaks in Switzerland) it was a life of respectable comfort and privilege that the educated elite of the eighties enjoyed. I was one of the lucky kids in school who had a room all to herself, unlike some of my classmates who grew up sleeping on a rolled-up bedding in their drawing room and had no money to spare for birthday treats – like Sangita. Probably one of the reasons why she had been driven to academic achievement at a very young age. Besides the fact that she always had a complex about her looks, of course.

Nana drove us around in a light green Fiat (Premier Padmini) on our many picnics, family dinners and sometimes even all the way to Tirupattur, our ancestral hometown in Tamil Nadu where Amma's elders stayed. Nana, having being orphaned at a very young age, was zealous about family. Even the family idiots – mentally unhinged and demented relatives – became revered stars, whose stories and anecdotes we were regaled with over and over again. It was fun.

At these happy times I often wondered if my head was making up stories of Amma's strictness to appease my own flaws and failings. And then again when Amma went back to her strict, rigid ways I would start to wonder if the happiness had been a dream after all.

Life oscillated wildly between the fragrance of heaven and the stench of hell. One day, full of laughs and love, the next, fraught with unreasonable expectations and incredible spite. We were never sure which way the pendulum would swing. Between these confounding variables I struggled to keep up the pretence of normalcy, living a life of lies masquerading as morality, taking refuge in music, theatre and other extra-curricular activities that I excelled at. Awards and medals that got me so much praise and attention from the outside world, that I could ignore the painful knots my adolescent feelings were turning into.

I was getting addicted to applause; my self-worth coming to be based entirely on the number of certificates, prizes, and trophies I collected. I even made a secret corner in my cupboard for all of them and would take them out often, boasting shamelessly, especially to my middle sister, Sunita, whom I had begun to look down upon because of her lack of attestations from the outside world. Much in the way Amma looked down on me because my marks weren't in the top five.

If my put-downs hurt Sunita she never mentioned it. And when she did occasionally express her concern that I couldn't look beyond my accomplishments, my condescension for her lack of certificate-acquiring abilities only increased. She smiled. It made me bully her even more.

Because of Nana's position and Amma's qualifications, doors

opened for me without my knowing or asking. Sometimes much against my wishes, for this often outshone the praise I got for any of my individual talents or achievements.

'What does it matter if you won the first prize at the interschool singing competition three years in a row? It's because of all this that your academic marks are coming down. Next time no taking part, understand?'

Keen to avoid the confrontations and the belligerence, I started withholding information from my parents. Refusing to inform them that I was participating in yet another music competition or school play or debate or indeed anything else I did. My joys and Amma-Nana's wishes were glaringly incompatible.

'Don't tell lies all the time, Chitty. What is the need to hide things from us? Can you imagine my embarrassment when Mrs Aulakh asked me why I didn't come for your singing competition last week where you sang so beautifully that you got a standing ovation?'

Ouch! Mean girl! a little voice in my head scolded. *Making Amma cry.* Why didn't you call her for your singing competition? Aren't you grateful for the beautiful voice you inherited from her? Shouldn't you be thanking her for it instead of causing her shame?

I had started forging my parents' signatures in my school diary too. Being punished by my teachers for my disobedience and rebellion was becoming an everyday affair. I could put up with the teachers' slaps and scoldings for another few months before I escaped to the next standard. But from Amma and Nana there was no escape – their memory of my wrongdoings, fanatical. Evasion, avoidance, forgery and bribe were easier options. If there was a god I would pray harder at the next pooja – he was bound to understand. I would explain my position and demand forgiveness.

Still, despite my resentment and growing anger I somehow knew my Amma was special; she was not like the other Ammas who played cards all day, spent all their time grooming themselves at beauty parlours, or feeding their families with traditional 'passed-down-through-the-generations' home-made delicacies. And so, because deep down I knew I had such a 'special-but-unacknowledged-by-the-world' Amma, every time people's eyes widened when I told them Nana was Commissioner of Income Tax, I would append my mother's job and qualifications to the standard, 'What-does-your-father-do-beta?' question that they would inevitably ask. Back in those days people rarely asked what your mother did. It was assumed a mother only mothered, and that was enough; so I would boast, 'My mother is the head of the department of History and a triple PhD.'

As in most South Indian homes, we too had a great big pooja platform. An ornate one with idols and pictures of all the Hindu gods and goddesses. Nana performed a little prayer ceremony every day, smearing four fingers of vibhuti (holy ash) across his forehead before leaving for work. On religious or festive days the drill was more elaborate and involved all of us. New clothes, oil baths and religious fasts. Today had been one of them. Saraswati Pooja – to pay obeisance to the goddess of learning. And I had sullied it.

'But I was hungry, Amma. There was nothing to eat in the fridge.'

'So what? You could have waited till I got back home. Don't even try and speak to me for a week. And yes, no going down to play, either. You have to stay in your room till your punishment is over. And if you continue to be disobedient and arrogant I will not talk to you for a month!'

'Nana, why don't you say something? Do you think Amma is being fair?'

'Every family has its own rules, kanna. They must be obeyed.'

We lived by the AEIOU rule – encompassing all the vowels on the alphabet scale. A diagram Amma had drawn up *All* By Herself and thrust down our throats with her iron fist, *All* the Time:

(A) Academics and
(E) Elders' Glorification
(I) Imposed by
(O) Obedience to
(U) Ultimatums.

'Your mother has sacrificed a lot of her own needs and desires for her children. Show some respect,' my father invariably said.

'So what? I didn't ask her to. How is it *my* fault? I am not just your daughter, I am a person, an individual; you need to show me some respect too.'

Individualism was a cancer. Non-conformism – the immoral conduct of sinners and no-gooders out to shame the great Indian middle-class family. Punishable by slaps, confinement, and infinite other forms of emotional cruelty. Elders were gods – to be worshipped. Disobedience of that diktat, blasphemy.

'You should obey your mother. Don't forget you're a good girl from a good family and don't shame us again by exposing your bare shoulders to the world like you did in that Clearasil skin cream commercial. That is the behaviour of prostitutes. If you want to do things behind your parents' back, you better get out of the house.'

'I have no choice *but* to do things behind your back, Amma. Because I don't find anything wrong in what I am doing but you want to make me feel ashamed of every thought and action of mine. And I will get out of this wretched house. You wait and see!'

'You should feel lucky with all the opportunities you have. If I had the kind of opportunities you have been given, I would have conquered the world.'

Yeah, yeah – how many times do I have to hear your Sad Sack stories, Amma? Of how being the great mother you are, you waited till your youngest-born was six before you resumed your education, which had been so brutally cut off in the tenth standard at the age of fifteen, in spite of your brilliance? By your father, who believed that girls should not become too clever because, otherwise, they wouldn't be able to adjust to their husbands?

'Is that why you forced Sujata to do home science instead of medicine or dentistry? So she would serve no man other than her husband?'

'Shut up! We did not force her. She herself was too lazy.'

'Rubbish. You twist everything to justify your own guilt. No wonder you're a triple PhD in history. A subject that I believe closes people's minds to actual reality and keeps it stuck in the quagmire of the past.'

'History is the foundation on which the future of the world is built.'

'What world, Amma? The world of *Aiyyo*'s and MBA's is not for me. And I cannot build a future on your history. I'm entitled to creating one of my own.'

I was sick of the smothering moral hypocrisy that so-called good families hid under. At the grandfather who ran behind servants squeezing their bums, or the beady-eyed uncle who tried to play footsie with his teenaged niece.

'*Aiyyo*, Nana. Chitty needs psychiatric counselling. Look at the way she is lying just to malign her elders. Aren't you going to do something?'

'Why don't *you* do something about the fact that Shambu Chinayna tried to play footsie with me at the dinner table yesterday and kept staring at my breasts?'

'*You* must have done something to invite that sort of attention. Maybe he saw that shameless photograph of yours in the magazine exposing your whole body in the Clearasil ad.'

'I did not expose my whole body. It was an off-shoulder top, that's all.'

'Go to your room, Chitty, and stay there till you learn to speak properly to your mother who has sacrificed so much for the sake of her children. If you don't behave I am going to stop your pocket money.'

'I don't need your stupid pocket money any more, Nana. I earn a thousand times that in five minutes by just flashing a smile at the camera. I only continue to take the pocket money you give me so that you don't feel bad.'

'Using your feminine charms to earn money is the way of prostitutes. If you can't obey your mother you better get out of the house...'

'Mummy has emasculated you, Nana. A father has to protect his children – but you're only concerned about Amma.'

'Don't talk to your parents like that, Chittappa,' Neelawwa, my grandmom advised gently. She was an angel. My one chance of trying to stay sane in that madhouse.

'Why not? If they can keep telling me I'm behaving like a prostitute because I'm modelling...?'

'They are just conservative. But good people. It is the culture they grew up in.'

But this was Metropolitan Mumbai – not a village in South India! Hadn't my parents figured that out yet?

In spite of their education and qualifications, Amma's and Nana's minds had remained locked in the barbaric misogyny of their village upbringing. Where disobedient wives were stripped and beaten. Where husbands who kept their wives pregnant year after year saw nothing wrong in seeking the company of prostitutes – sometimes even squandering away family wealth and leaving their families in penury for it. Where women were beaten for uttering simple words or threatened with having their tongues cut off for laughing too loud. Where girls fortunate enough to be allowed an education after puberty never ventured out without carrying chilli powder in their hands to frighten away molesters.

'Who has told you all this rubbish, Chitty? Our life in the village was peaceful and beautiful. Something that you can't imagine. Stop trying to malign your family.'

'You're the ones who told me these stories.' Had Amma and Nana forgotten already? How on earth could I have made up things so bizarre?

And so my parents unthinkingly, unconsciously imposed

on us the age-old biases, discriminations, and fears that clouded their minds. Glorifying the very culture that they once themselves had fled from. In a bid perhaps to reduce the stifling alienation they now experienced in the big city.

But as an adolescent I didn't empathize with any of this. My rebellion was far greater than my understanding. Why teach children to be honest, inquisitive and just, if you couldn't be that way yourself? Why teach them to think, if you are so afraid of their thoughts? And why punish them only because they didn't mirror yours?

♋

One day my friend Monica came home dressed in shorts. We were all of twelve years old. Amma asked, 'Why is your friend wearing such a *chaddi choomchee* dress?'

'*Chaddi choomchee*' can be loosely translated as 'ass-revealing'. Amma asked Monica to go home and change into something more decent and then come back. Obviously, Monica never did. And she stopped speaking to me forever, for no fault of mine. Even Monica's mother roamed around in shorts, for god's sake – no big deal. She even came to school in them. Why were my folks so paranoid about bared flesh?

Neelawwa's response was always to twist her fingers upwards in a mudra and hug me tight. My grandmother had no other answer. It was the 187th time she had done this – (I kept count in my diary.)

'I know why they are so paranoid, Neelawwa. Because they are so obsessed with sex that in their heads even a flower looks like a vagina. A finger, a penis…'

'*Aiyyo*, Chittappa. Calm down, ra kanna,' my grandmother

would plead. 'Nobody is so bad. Try to see it from their point of view.'

No way! I was done with their point of view. I was going to have it *my* way. I was going to be in the movies and be a star. That would be my revenge.

But my battleship on the journey to stardom was fragile and the ride so choppy I often feared it would capsize and I would go down with it. Struggling to counter the I-told-you-so, finger-wagging warnings of my parents with the shady cloak-and-dagger shenanigans of the film world was doubly confounding for me.

'Suchitra, you want to be an actress, you must *do*...'

'Do? Do *what*?'

I could never figure out the code of conduct that newbies in showbiz were bound to follow by some unwritten law. It was the 'they' syndrome all over again.

'Do. All actresses – they *do*. They must *do*. Where are your parents? You phone them just now. I'll explain it to them.'

Oh no! Had he guessed my runaway status, the fact that I was living on my own?

'Erm...my parents will be in office now...I can't disturb them...'

'Okay, no problem. Phone them later. Who are you more close to – your mother or father?'

'My father. Amma is a little strict but Nana is very kind...'

'So will you phone your Nana in the evening and tell him to pick you up from my hotel tomorrow morning?

Tomorrow morning? What was I supposed to do till then? The old geezer was stodgy as hell. Had body odour, too. He was boring me already.

'Where are you running away, child? I told you to be an actress you must *do*. Now relax...'

Oh really? Do *him*? Boo Hoo.

Doobey doobey doo.

And *fuck you*!

Unlike all the other girls of that era who were accompanied on the set by their mummies – I went alone. And continued to hide the fact that I lived alone from everybody in the movie business. Telling everyone that my parents were working people and were therefore too busy to follow me around.

It wasn't long before I started to react with petulant derision to anything I was told.

'Why should I pad my bra with mounds of stiff cotton under my dress?' I mean, how were big boobs connected with acting prowess? These people were mental or what?

'Suchitra, your forehead is looking too big. We need to get you a fringe...' No way – I would promptly instruct the hairdresser to pull my hair back as far as possible and pin it tight.

'Suchitra, we need to shoot with you tomorrow...'

'Sorry, I'm not free. I have to meet my boyfriend.'

'You have a *boyfriend*?'

Back then, in the early nineties – that coy, pretend era of 35-year-old actresses claiming to be saving their hymens for their husbands-to-be – a teen admitting that she had a boyfriend was unusual. A shocker.

My boyfriend was, of course, Shekhar Kapur whom I would phone every evening during the shooting of *Kabhi Haan Kabhi Naan* in Goa, regaling him with the day's proceedings and other random musings. Sometimes wondering aloud to him why film folk seemed so different from regular folk. Like, why I was refused a Coca Cola on the set on a day when the temperature had soared to scorching. I was almost fainting in the heat, for god's sake. What was their problem? I was just asking for a soft drink, not the moon. And then when I had insisted on paying for it because I so badly needed one, the animosity had only seemed to worsen – the Coca Cola still denied.

'My boyfriend says that it's because people in the movies mostly come from poor backgrounds and are not used to drinking Coca Cola or owning a car or...'

'Suchitra, don't tell anyone you have a boyfriend! Actresses should be unattached or producers are wary of signing them. You are not planning to get married, are you?'

Of course I planned to get married. I was a good girl from a good family – who did they think I was?

'But your career will be ruined!'

'Career? Why did people talk only about a career? Didn't they understand *anything* about love?

All By Myself
Don't wanna be – All By Myysellfff!
Any Moooooorre!!

Celine Dion's stricken, high-pitched, seizure-inducing soprano playing on a loop, slapped me back to the present. 'Yes, Amma. You're right. I ruined my life because I married Shekhar only for sex.'

'Shut up, Chitty. If you're going to talk to your mother like this I'm going to put the phone down. Don't think I don't know how you tricked Shekhar into marrying you. By pretending to be a good girl from a good family – poor fellow. He thought he will never otherwise be able to have sex with you. I am your mother – you cannot fool me.'

'That's exactly what I'm saying. That I married Shekhar only for sex and now I want to marry again only for sex…Chitty Chitty – *Bang Bang*…'

'Shut up and don't be disgusting. You can marry a Hindu also, even if it's only for sex. If you think you can marry a Muslim and get away with it, it's your funeral. But remember, that if you do that I will not be your mother any more. Understood?'

Boy oh boy, wouldn't *that* be a relief? With Amma no longer obliged to fulfil her maternal duties I would finally be liberated! I would not have to spend all my alimony on visiting shrinks and going for calming ayurvedic massages and Reiki and deep-tissue healing. I could use all that saved-up money to travel to exotic foreign places, to have glorious holiday romances with tall, dark and handsome strangers. Shamelessly and excessively. Go crazy *and* kinky. I wouldn't have to worry about finding myself a husband *or* about Amma's disapproving gaze branding me a prostitute. Aaaaah, delicious! Glorious, born-again me!

I turned off my iPod. *Phew!* What a relief!

My spirits started to soar. I was going to shrug off my woes in no time. I knew it! The solution had always been so simple – why on earth hadn't I seen it all along?

A person is not technically born till the umbilical cord is cut, dig?

'I still say you better marry Shekhar only. You're not getting any younger you know, and you're losing your looks too with all your bad habits.'

'Crap, Amma. I have friends who are still single or just pregnant for the first time.'

'Yes, I know. I have met your recent circle of friends...All spinsters and divorcees. Birds of a feather will always flock together. And some of them are so ugly...which man will marry them? You better stop this nonsense and do some work. Why are you not painting these days? And don't you have any film offers? What about that Ram Gopal Varma chap? Why don't you contact him again? He extracted a good performance from you in that Amitabh Bachchan movie...can't remember the name...'

'*Rann.*'

'Yes, *Rann.* I think that is the best solution for you instead of "I want to marry this Iqbal" nonsense and calling up your poor old mother in the middle of the night. Ram Gopal Varma is Telugu like us – he will surely help you.'

Telugu like us? Oh, so we were Telugu now and not Tamil? How convenient and mind-boggling was that? Like the adiabatic expansion of water that contracts to make ice – and then, for reasons no one knows, expands suddenly to crack the very glass it's set in. It's what Amma's blasé oxymorons did to my brain – shrunk it into frozen ice till it made my fragile-as-glass skull crack and explode in protest.

My mother-tongue has always been one of the great mysteries of my life. We spoke Telugu at home as did all my relatives. Nana said we are Telugu but Amma insisted that we were Tamil.

I tried to clarify our status with Nana. 'You mean you are Telugu and Amma's Tamil? Like interstate marriage and all?'

'No, we are both Telugu,' Nana would explain. 'But she did

her schooling in the Tamil language and lived in Tamil Nadu so…'

'So?'

'And my Telugu ancestors settled in Telangana district when both states i.e. Tamil Nadu and Andhra Pradesh were one so…'

'Whatever, Nana. Just tell me how that makes us Tamil?'

'It doesn't. We are Telugu.'

'But *Amma* says…' *Uff!* My brain had shown signs of cracking as early as age nine – just like the adiabatic expansion of water. I struggled with ways to keep it unfrozen, so that it wouldn't splinter, shatter, and spew its contents on the drawing room floor.

When asked to state my mother-tongue in school forms I simply wrote English.

'English cannot be your mother-tongue, Suchitra. Stop being silly.'

'Why not? I think in English, I am being educated in English, and so English is my mother-tongue.'

'Get out of the class. You are punished for two whole periods.'

'You better call Ram Gopal Varma – ' Amma chided me over the telephone line. 'And ask him to give you some decent roles. And always remember before doing any nonsense that you're a mother! Now good night. Oh, before I put the phone down, what happened to that Gangotri chap?'

'What Gangotri chap?' I didn't know any Gangotri chap.'

'That Gangotri chap who's been coming and playing Scrabble with you for the last two years?'

'Not Gangotri. Ganatra. Pankaj Ganatra.'

'Whatever. I hope you have not given in to his advances?'

'What advances, Amma? Are you mad? We just love to play Scrabble.'

'Are you so dumb, ra kanna? Do you think a man will come and play Scrabble with you so often if he has no ulterior motive? Does he not have any other work? I hope you are not drinking wine and taking drugs in his presence. I don't trust that chap. These business people are cunning. All they have is money, no education. And men try to get girls drunk only because alcohol makes people loose and immoral. I'm sure he's telling you that his marriage is not working because his wife doesn't understand him. Married men are the most shameless. You of all the people should know that...'

'Amma, please. He's a friend who loves to play Scrabble just like me, and that's all. We don't talk about his marriage or mine and I don't do drugs. And we don't drink wine while playing Scrabble because it disturbs the concentration.'

But the truth was Pankaj's marriage was treading rocky terrain. And although he never talked about it I kind of sensed what was going on…but... hitting on me? Naah. Pankaj was too sensible to ever try that 'my-marriage-is-on-the-rocks' line with me. He knew me well enough – the fact that I'm a *good* girl from a *good* family (ha ha). He was one of the few male buddies I had left in a life filled with women – girlfriends, gal pals and my gaggle of girlies whom I was sick of hugging just to feel some love and warmth in my life. Pankaj was certainly no stalker or grabber in waiting. I was safe.

And, my god, *what* a pleasure it was to hug someone with no squishy-squashy breasts! How I longed for the hardness of that embrace. Since I didn't know any woman without breasts, Pankaj was currently my only chance of contact with a non-breasted body. Hugging men is as vital as hanging with girlfriends. Why was Amma trying to make me feel guilty for the simple pleasures of life all over again? I'd even told Pankaj to find me a husband – he'd promised me he was on the look-out.

'Okay, goodnight. I'll pray to god to give you buddhi. You be careful. I'm still telling you, your best bet is Shekhar – after all he is the father of your child. And take my advice and call Ram Gopal Varma tomorrow. He will definitely help you. And please remember, before doing anything stupid that you're first and foremost a mother! Your main duty is towards your child. I have sacrificed everything so that my children can be happy. Don't let it go waste. Good night.'

♋

Depressing as it was, and as conversations with Amma invariably turned out, she had set my mind racing. I paced the room feverishly thinking maybe I did have a plan. Ramu a.k.a Ram Gopal Varma had always been super-kind to me. Constantly complimenting me on my camera-friendly face and histrionic talent. In fact, a few years ago, when my marriage was falling apart and I had decided to move back to Mumbai from London, starting to look for work as an actress, Ramu was the only one who hadn't asked, 'Won't Shekhar have objections to you acting again, Suchitra?'

The chauvinism of the people in the Hindi movie industry was truly appalling! How come nobody had ever asked me if *I* had any objection to the things Shekhar had done, did, continued to do, and was sure to do in the future?

So, relieved and grateful when Ramu had fished out a script at our very first meeting in many years and bashfully asked, 'It's not a very big role, Suchitra, but a very powerful one. Read the script and see if you'd like to do it...' I had immediately said yes. The film was *My Wife's Murder*, with Anil Kapoor. I played Sheila, Anil Kapoor's nagging shrew of a wife who in the film is – yup, you guessed right – murdered! By her very own husband! *Tan de daaaan!*

I got raves for that performance too – being lauded as a great actress. Of course I didn't tell anyone that there was no acting required for that particular role. I was merely imitating my mother, ha ha.

And so I thought Amma's suggestion that I should call Ramu now – once again at a crisis-point in my life – was a fantastic one. A master idea bordering on sheer genius! Voila! What a breakthrough! For the first time in my life I had to acknowledge the fact that Amma's nonsense occasionally did make sense.

So as soon as I hung up the phone I fished out my diary and altered my next day's schedule from:

- Do pranayama deep breathing.
- Go for meditation class at Ina's at 12.
- Send three anxiety candles to Simran who is going through a tough time with her divorce.
- Send dogs with maid to vet for flea treatment.
- Pick up Kaveri from birthday party at 7.

to:

- Do pranayama deep breathing.
- Go to Ina's for meditation at 12.

- Send three anxiety candles to Simran who is going through a tough time with her divorce.
- Send dogs with maid to vet for flea treatment.
- Pick up Kaveri from birthday party at 7 and help with her paper pulp bowl project.
- Call Shekhar for lawyer's number.
- Speak to lawyer and file suit against Shrink and Celine Dion.
- Send a pack of Pampers to Sangita.
- Send sms to Ramu and fix up a meeting.

3

I slept like a baby the moment my head hit the pillow. I couldn't remember the last time I had woken up feeling so well rested and refreshed. From this day on I was going to be a brand new person *and* I intended to make it all happen for myself with no assistance whatsoever from god, girlfriends or Ganatras.

It was time to execute the next and most important plan of the day – and for the rest of my life.

I dressed. Put on some make-up and waited till it was office opening time. To calm my nerves, I lit my anxiety candle and inhaled deeply. God this candle was good – I was a genius. It was time I recognized this and stopped beating myself up for no reason. My anxiety candle calmed me down in a jiffy. One day, I thought, when I was once again well settled, radiant in the glow of my new marriage and the bliss of my domestic life, newborn twins in tow, I would send out my life-saving anxiety candles into the world. With a fine marketing plan that my brilliant husband had set up, of course. After all, I dimpled happily, men are *so* much better at organizing stuff and negotiating deals. My candles would retail and sell in stores all over the world and soon I would be gloriously rich and famous, straddling and balancing both, material and marital nirvana. All done the completely natural and holistic way. And I would flaunt my success and wealth to my girlfriends. So Sangita would understand that a woman doesn't have to be in an office, wear pants and grow a moustache to be rich and successful. And it would finally dawn on Chandni that I would rather spend all my resources healing the world from anxiety and other emotional disorders than buying myself a Gucci handbag.

And their boasting and brain-chewing would stop once and for all. Oh, and yes, all this would be mine just by staying home and doing the things I loved to do as a woman. No need for the kind of aggro and jealous competitiveness they shoved down my throat every day

I steadied myself. *Whoa!* Calm down, Suchitra. One step at a time. All this is round the corner. For now, the immediate moment – it's time to send that life-changing sms to Ramu.

Yes, yes – right on the button, Einstein. It was 10.15 a.m. Most people reach their work places by around 10 a.m. and start attending to emails and sms's shortly thereafter. Purrfect! With trembling fingers and a thudding heart I typed the sms that I yearningly imagined would transform my life and catapult me out of my loneliness into blessed holy matrimony. With a Telugu, no less! Oh, my parents would finally feel pleased with something I had done! And my dilemma about whether I was Tamil or Telugu would be resolved once and for all. I mean, once I marry a Telugu I would automatically be declared a Telugu, *na*?

I concentrated hard – couldn't afford spelling mistakes now could I? Like that invite for the painting exhibition that socialite had sent me, full of typos – how pathetic was that! And she had the gall to ask me why I didn't show up to support her tackiness. *Uff!*

I read, reread, and once again scrutinized the sms with alert, newly-awakened, hawk eyes to make sure I had got it right. It was perfect. Purrfect!

'Ramu will you marry me?'

I read it again.

How cool an sms *was* that?

Modern men like bold women with a direct approach.

I was on target. Bingo!

I pressed send.

Phew! There! It was done. Not so difficult, after all. I applauded my own courage and treated myself to three Snicker bars, a packet of banana chips and a mango sorbet as a reward. I would go on a diet later and lose the weight in time for the marriage ceremony. Wow. Thrilling! Finally my life was in my own hands and nobody could stop me.

Ever again.

Not my mother, not my father, not my ex husband (even though I did let him talk me out of filing a lawsuit against Celine Dion, because, like Shekhar explained, I had no case there. Because, well, apparently, legally, artists have a right to express themselves. So if her song '*All By Myself*' was upsetting me so much and making me gosh darn near suicidal, I should have turned off my iPod earlier. Made sense, *na*? *Hmm*...)

♋

While I waited for Ramu's reply I binged on some more banana chips and did some more pranayama breathing. Several hours passed by. I spent the time inhaling deeply the aromas of my anxiety candle, and simultaneously soaking newspapers in water and Fevicol for Kaveri's paper pulp, papier mache project.

It was too early in the day for a glass of wine (only alcoholics drink during the day!) And since I don't do drugs – regardless of what Amma thinks – I decided I would pop a bottle of champagne when this cat and mouse marriage proposal game was behind me – when I lay blissfully naked and satiated in my husband's arms. (*Chheh! Chheh!* Why are you thinking about things like *naked? Shameless girl!*)

I waited. I was willing to give Ramu time. After all, marriage was a serious thing – he was probably just as nervous as I was. Perhaps he hadn't received my text message in spite of the 'D' report on my phone.

D for delivered.
D for daring.
D for damn cool!

Perhaps the reason for Ramu's silence was something as simple as the fact that he had changed his telephone and not transferred his old contact list. So maybe my name hadn't registered on the new instrument? Celebrities have to be careful, you know, of whom they communicate with. Too many psychos in the world. I've had that experience myself. Even getting calls from pimps offering me vulgarly huge sums of money to sleep with filthy rich, adulterous men.

This had actually happened a few years ago, back when my divorce drama had dominated the headlines in Indian newspapers for what had seemed like an eternity. Can you imagine, this third-class pimp had the bloody guts to tell me, 'I know you're a good girl, madam. But NRI (Non Resident Indian) party very pucca. Solid. And they also want a good girl only. Nobody but you, madam...'

'They want a good girl and so you're calling me to prostitute myself, you arsehole?!' I was trembling with shocked outrage.

'Don't get upset, madam. Try and understand. I know you're not like that. That's why party wants good girl like you only, madam. You're also Shekhar Kapur's wife, madam. High status. You name your price. And then if you want I can negotiate an even higher rate for you...'

Since Mr. Pimp had been calling from an unknown/private number there had been no method to track him down and report him to the cops. Dang! How I would have enjoyed unleashing Amma on Mr Pimp to abuse him in Telugu while he rotted in jail. Instead, I had been left with no choice but to change my number.

So...umm...could it be...had Ramu's number changed too? Is *that* why there was still no response to my marriage proposal? I made a few enquiries surreptitiously. With friends and colleagues who were sure to have Ramu's new number even if it had changed. Turned out I had the right one – no worries on *that* account.

More time went by. Dang! I was starting to get very agitated. Still no reply! Why, why, why? Was it because I had sent him that nasty letter telling him why I didn't like *'Rann'* and how ugly I thought I looked in it? That I wished he had lit my face better, rather than focusing all the lights on the other actress's underwear? Naah...Ramu was a mature man. Open to criticism. He always told me my viewpoint was fresh and unique. That I should write more. He wasn't likely to be annoyed about that letter for too long. If he was, it would have shown up in the sms's or conversations I'd had with him since then, wouldn't it? Or would it not? Had I misunderstood it all?

Oh no – I felt my brain turning all confused again. *Breathe in, breathe out. Breathe in, breathe out!*

The wait was nerve-wracking. I paced up and down the house, I climbed into bed, I tossed and turned and twisted and swivelled. Round and round, in cartwheels of mounting anxiety. What was happening to me? I checked my phone every few minutes. Dawn to dusk, day to night, but still no reply in sight.

Sigh! Another long, insomniacal night.

Clearly, my insomnia candle was not as effective as my anxiety candle. Which, as I have already shared with you, is super-effective in quelling palpitations, phobias and other 'I'm-so-afraid-of-my-life' murmurs. I knew I had to alter the formula for the insomnia one, but what to do? How could I? The other essential-oil ingredient that was supposed to be a sure-shot remedy for sleeplessness was a bloody 70,000 bucks a kg, or some such appalling price. What would I tell Kaveri, whom I had promised to send to London for the Diwali holidays so she could spend time with her friend Alisha – 'Sorry, my baby, no foreign holiday for you, okay? I spent too much of my alimony on essential-oils this month. We'll go to Bangalore instead to visit Ammama Thatha. And we'll go by train! Second-class sleeper unreserved!' *Uff!*

I would have to have a word with Shekhar about this. Not about my marriage proposal to Ramu, obviously, but about Kaveri. She was getting a bit too spoilt. I needed to make her more grounded,. Get her adapted to a more middle-class mindset. Not the 'sex is a sin', 'all actresses are prostitutes' and 'get out of the house' kind of whacked-out middle-class twistees, but just in terms of economics. What was the need for a ten-year-old to fly first class? If Shekhar was so particular about his daughter, why wasn't he around to take her to the dentist's to have her cavities filled? And then – just to boast to the dentist about what sterling richness and high falutin class he had – he could have her cavity filled with 24 carat gold, topped with an ice-cube-sized pink diamond solitaire.

Oh no! What was I thinking? That would make it impossible for my baby to close her mouth and give her pain and flies would enter and...OMG! What a *horrible* person I was! Mother Evil! God, please forgive me! My poor baby! How is any of this her fault? What can Kaveri do if her best friend owns thirteen cars including a Mercedes, a BMW and a Jaguar? Or for that matter, what could I do, either? How was I supposed to compete with that? Now you understand why I needed a husband so bad?

Aiyyo! Don't tell anybody about what you just thought, Suchitra. Keep pretending that it's all for love and companionship and bringing more beautiful babies into this world – just like Kaveri. Okay? Because it was entirely true that Ramu a.k.a Ram Gopal Varma didn't have the kind of wealth that some of Kaveri's classmates had. But, since I hadn't thought about this important fact before sending him the marriage proposal sms this morning, I now had no choice but to marry him.

It's okay, Suchitra. A wife is Laxmi – the goddess of wealth. Your entry into his life as his beautiful bride will catapult him into the ozone league of riches. I dreamed a dream of wearing a crown (Just like Goddess Laxmi) and floating in a golden chariot in the clouds. I imagined fanning myself with peacock feathers and blowing kisses to those mere mortals – (translated as my jealous girlfriends) who were craning their necks in awestruck wonder, just to catch a glimpse of me.

It was the thunderstorm threatening to crash-land my

floating pagoda into the jagged mountains that forced me to open my eyes.

It was 11. 30 a.m. – Dang! Half my morning was gone. I could have sent Ramu another 15 sms's by now. If only I had managed to wake up in time for office opening hours. So, in order to not waste any more precious time, I rephrased the sms I had sent yesterday to: *'Hi Ramu. Will you marry me? Suchitra Krishxxx'*

Now he couldn't possibly mistake it for anyone else's even if he hadn't stored my number in his new phone.

And, then, in a frantic, sleep-deprived, catatonic haze, I hit the send key again.

♋

My phone beeped at 11.47 a.m. sharp. Yes! Yes! *Yes!* It was him! He had responded. God is great.

'Hi Suchitra. Will be in my office by 2. Why don't you drop by for a cup of tea around 3?'

'Can we make it 4 Ramu?' (*Never* seem too eager and *never* run immediately when a man calls. Men love a challenge.) *'I have an important meeting at 3 – will come directly from there'.*

'Ok, c u'. End of text. Conversation over. *Soo* busy.

I was elated. *Yippee!* Happy days were here again. 'You Are My Sunshine, you are my…'

I wish I had managed to sleep a little more, though. The shadows under my eyes were a dark grey, bordering on black. So what? Nothing that a little artful makeup would not conceal. And hollowed-out eyes are a sign of intelligence and deep thinking, Suchitra. So chill. Better to reveal your dark circles than your deep cleavage, Amma always said.

I planned to keep the dressing sober and casual, even though I did call Rubina the hairdresser immediately for a hair fix. Can't talk marriage looking like golliwog, *na*? The maid barged in halfway through my blow-dry with a large bouquet of carnations and a handwritten note on scented paper and some printed shit.

'How many times do you have to be told that you need to knock before you enter? Doesn't that big fat salary I pay you from my hard-earned alimony deserve even an iota of obedience? Ungrateful wretch!'

'Sorry, madam – Chandni madam has sent these for you.'

I looked at the note. The bloody paper looked more expensive than the house I lived in. *Uff!* Why did Chandni always flaunt her wealth and penchant for fine living when she knew very well how badly I wanted to buy that insomnia-oil but couldn't afford to? The crafty use of words in her childish scrawl made it all the more obvious: 'Dearest Suchitra, these flowers are from me and Sangita. I'm sorry about our spat last night...'

Sorry, my arse. Wait till I get married. Then I will get rid of you once and for all from my life without worrying about having nothing else to do or no one else to talk to...

'I know you're depressed. We perfectly understand.'

Oh no, you don't understand at all, my irritating girlfriend; co-conspirator to my misery with my even more irritating girlfriend, Sangita. I am not *depressed. I just want to get married to avoid the company of the likes of the two of you, and fill my life with more meaningful pursuits than buying designer handbags for 5 lakhs, or learning about the effects of jojoba oil night-cream for super-moisturized pubic skin. Don't patronize me, understand?*

I wanted to scream. I should have never given her Shrink's

telephone number or ever shared with her the top-secret that I was seeing one. She was using it to blackmail me and suck me back into her vacuous, stupid, low-IQ world. Bloody brainless vampire.

The note continued. 'We love you and will always be there to help. Am sending you a printout of a Stanford University survey that I downloaded from the internet last night...'

Chandni's handwriting looked like she hadn't studied beyond the fifth standard even though I knew for a fact that she was a twelfth standard fail.

'When you read the teachings of the Stanford University survey you'll understand and appreciate the importance of girlfriends in your life. We need to stick by each other...'

I smelt something burn. '*Ouch!* You're holding the dryer too close to my scalp, Rubina! What are you trying to do? Burn my scalp and make me bald so nobody marries me? Has Chandni paid you to fry my brain?'

What kind of conniving treachery was this now?

I read the note as Rubina finished my blow dry.

Mind-Body connection – the relationship between stress and disease: Among other things, one of the best things a man can do for his health is to be married to a woman.'

This was useful and potentially potent ammunition…it may come in use later in the afternoon. Would keep it mind and fire the scientific survey cannon at precisely the right moment if required. I read on:

'Whereas for a woman one of the best things to do for her health is to nurture the relationship with her girlfriends. Women connect with each other differently and provide support systems that help each other deal with stress and difficult life experiences. Physically

'girlfriend time' helps us to create serotonin – a neurotransmitter that combats depression and creates a general feeling of well-being.

Bollocks! Who the hell wanted serotonin from hugging girlfriends? I was *soo* sick of that. I would gladly trade dollops of serotonin for a smidgeon of the endorphins one got from a romp in the hay any day.

'Women share feelings whereas men form relationships around activities. They rarely sit down with a buddy and talk about how they feel about certain things. Jobs? Yes. Fishing hunting golf? Yes. But their feelings? Rarely. Only women do that. They share their souls with their sister's mother's girlfriends and evidently that is very good for their soul.'

I snorted. My soul was fine. I had read enough books like *Seat of the Soul* by Gary Zukov and *Many Lives Many Masters*. It was only after I read *Living with the Devil* that I understood that there was no shame in being horny.

'Failure to create and maintain quality personal relationships with fellow humans is as dangerous as smoking! So every time you hang to schmooze with your girlfriends, pat yourself on the back for doing something good for your health.'

Hell, what I needed for my health right now was the complete opposite of the only thing I currently had in my life. That is, the company of my girlfriends. Girls, girls, and more girls. I hated all of them. Girlies with whom I spent every waking hour I could spare from my duties as a devoted mother. And for those few moments I needed to be by myself in solitary confinement to explore my existential angst without hearing about how sex would help me get rid of all my troubles – including my acne.

'Why don't you try it, at least for that reason, Suchitra? I swear all this is nothing but the disease of abstinence,' Chandni had gone on doggedly.

To Chandni it was my sword of Damocles. To me, I wished I had a sword right now to cut out her tongue that spoke of nothing but body fixes. How about the brain, duh? Huh?

Because the human brain also needs a change every now and then. Just like the human body needs sex, sex, sex – like you keep harping on and I don't agree with. And because if you don't give me a breather, my girlfriend, my mental stimulation is going to stall and my body will begin to deteriorate and make me die and decompose in a fifth of the time that it otherwise takes the average human. Bloody going on and on about…

Christ! Chandni had even sent even a map with the printed literature to substantiate her girlfriends'-are-glorious gobbledook!

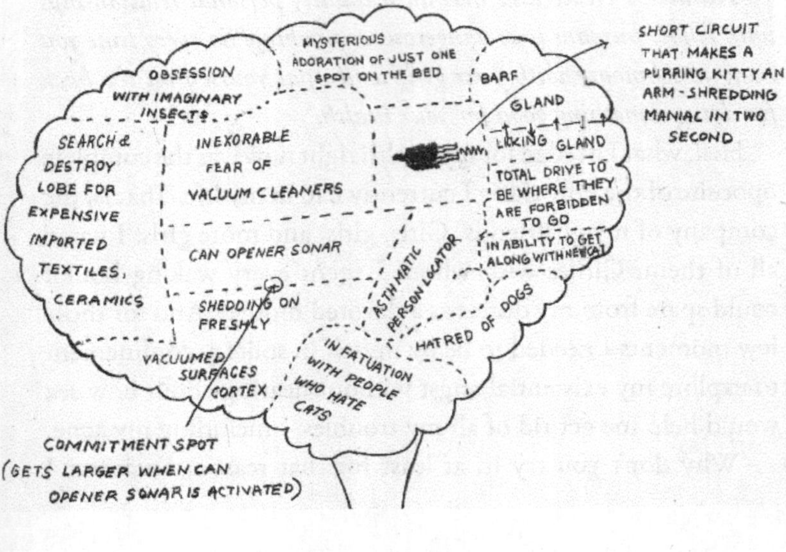

I decided that I would ask Ramu if he could help me out with just one more thing besides the happily-ever-after. I would ask if he could put me in touch with one of those gangsters whom he based his D company movies on. One of those guys who could issue warning/death/ *'keep-away-from-Suchitra-forever-if-you-want-to-stay-alive'* threats to Chandni and Sangita. I would be really grateful.

I would tell Ramu that it was crucial that this bribe be paid anonymously via his good offices, so that my name didn't figure anywhere. Can't afford incarceration, *na*? Who would look after Kaveri if her mother had to spend the next few years in jail?

If this had happened when Kaveri was older, like say when she was eighteen or twenty-one rather than ten or eleven, I would have done it myself without the aid of dodgy gangster types. Even if it meant the possibility of spending the rest of my life in prison. But right now I couldn't risk that. And I definitely had no time for this bonhomie of the babe's bunkum.

After all, I had the most important meeting for the rest of my happily-ever-after life to go to!

I stopped short. *Wait a minute.* Had my girlfriends placed a bug or a chip in my phone to spy on me? Had Chandni sent me this stupid Stanford university gibberish to derail me and thwart my marriage chances forever? The spot-on timing could not just be coincidence, could it?

Chandni was obviously desperate to retain me as a girlfriend after giving me all that blah about my rudeness. She must have guessed that I was planning to eliminate them from my space as soon as I found myself a husband. Devious, bloody creature. Forget it, I told myself – I would deal with the likes of her later.

So, attired in low-waist hipster jeans that I knew enhanced my figure – and Ramu does have a penchant for these things, lord knows – and a simple white tee, I strolled into his office wearing my most casual expression.

See, there are some great advantages to being an actress – no matter what one's state of mind, one can always manage to come up with a completely contrary expression on cue. You don't need the 'lights, camera, action' command. All you need to tell yourself is, *'one, two, three, pretend!'* And I had been practising this casual expression from 11.48 a.m. to 2.30 that afternoon – as soon as I had received his sms to come meet him – so I knew I had got it right.

Pankaj called just as I was about to enter Ramu's office. 'Am back from Bangkok tonight. Want to play Scrabble?'

What if Ramu had an objection to me scrabbling alone in the house with another man? It's natural for husbands – even the would-be ones – to be possessive about their wives, *na*?

'I'll let you know, Pankaj. I'll call you later, okay?'

4

'Suchitra! Come in, come in. You're looking beautiful as usual,' Ramu is the king of compliments

Thanks, Ramu. I should meet you more often. Sooo good for my self confidence. 'Hello – so nice to see you,' I purred throatily instead, extending my arms in a casual kinda hug.

Here I *have* to mention that Ramu is the worst hugger in the world. He just stands rod straight with his arms stiffly by his side…Oh god my choice of words! What I mean is that he stands like a cardboard mannequin (*There! That's better; more decent!*) and expects *you* to do all the hugging work. I've known him for almost forever years and he's always been like that. So, it was not that he had suddenly become shy and embarrassed because of my marriage proposal or something.

I don't know why he's such a bad hugger, though…is hugging a western Mumbai/Delhi type culture and not Hyderabad or pan Indian? Maybe Indians who grow up in smaller towns and villages don't hug that well? Or not at all? Perhaps they are more attuned to the clinical formality of a 'namaste', which immediately conveys good manners, humility and adherence to noble Indian values? Rather than having to make it obvious that what they are actually thinking with the namaste is, 'Stay away from me in case you have some kind of infectious disease like herpes, AIDS or rabies that is contracted from physical contact with other human bodies and animals.' *Hmm*...could be. Not sure. Or maybe hugging is an international phenomenon because, well, Pankaj travels a lot abroad and boy-o-boy is *he* a good hugger, or what? Make that fantastic. Makes Scrabble so so...so...*sigh!* I myself had learnt to hug properly only in the years I had lived in London.

Shush, Suchitra, I admonished myself. Why are you thinking of hugging another man in the presence of your soon-to-be husband and going all weird? Especially, as Amma had said, I had better beware of Pankaj. Because he travelled to Bangkok a lot – and everyone knows *that* city to be a den of prostitution. Really? OMG! If that was really true then it was good I said I would call him later instead of immediately agreeing to his diabolical Scrabble scheme. How could I even *think* of corrupting my pureness, which I was saving for my future husband, just so I could satisfy my insane urge to hug a body without tits? Besides, what I meant was that Pankaj's hugs made Scrabble s*oo*...erm…spiritual.

Spiritual. That's the word. Not sexy, okay? Do you get that, Chitty? *Slap! Whack! Dishoom!*

Can't afford to seem like a despo to Ramu – not at this crucial juncture of our twenty-odd years' on-and-off relationship, based *entirely* on his friendship with my ex-husband. But forget all that. Today it was vital that I came across as a decent girl from a decent family. What man would take home a slut? (Funny that whenever it comes to issues of morality I address myself by my pet name, 'Chitty' – because that's what my family calls me. When I talk to myself on other occasions I always address myself as Suchitra.)

I shuddered, trying to cover my desperate need for a hug – in danger of it being immediately recognized as an expression of unbridled, sexual-deprivation by Ramu's x-ray eyes. I grabbed his hand and shook it in what I considered a firm, robust handshake, placing my left palm over his right to complete the circle of warmth; revealing no signs whatsoever of inner frustration. Once again, my years of experience as an actress, enabling me to draw from deep inner resources to fake cool outer responses, holding me in good stead. So you see, what I conveyed just by the grip of my hand was not a 'hello-nice-to-meet-you' professional kinda vibe, but an 'OMG-Ramu-I'm-thrilled-to-see-you-after-so-long', fervent, 'warming-the-cockles-of-one's-heart' kind of one.

One day when we were married and had children and all, I would have to explain to him that a hug is not a sexual gesture but one of affection. For now, I dredged up the most sincere, asexual expression I could from the depths of my soul and into my eyes. This was as decent and clever as I could be right now, in spite of my raging inner demons. I think I pulled it off quite well too.

He didn't blink. 'How's Shekhar? Where is he these days? London? Los Angeles?'

'Why don't you call him and ask him yourself, Ramu?' I said a little peevishly. 'How would I know – we are divorced.'

'Chill, I know. Was just wondering what he's working on these days. That's all. Nothing personal.'

Chill, Suchitra, I told myself too. *You're overreacting.* But I'm bound to overreact, aren't I? Why does everybody keep asking me about Shekhar? Wasn't my present difficult enough? Why did Ramu have to remind me of my identity crisis of the past?

Still, I inhaled deeply and held my tongue in check, trying hard to not stare at Ramu's bulging biceps. Rudeness at this critical juncture would be nothing but self-destructive; a classic, dysfunctional family symptom brought on from years of abject hopelessness, which always prophesied failure. The deeply ingrained fear that what you're doing is never quite the right thing for yourself.

'*Don't blame your dysfunctional home for your stinking, puerile thoughts, Chitty. Always full of blame and revenge! You have had a perfect upbringing, so try to utilize your brilliant academic genes in a useful manner, rather than constantly blaming your parents for all the problems in your life! How would you feel if Kaveri accused you of the same thing?*

I mentally slapped my head. *Ouch!* How had Amma got into Ramu's office? Where was she hiding right now? Behind that hideous world map on the wall behind his desk? Was Amma upset that I had asked Ramu for his hand in marriage rather than a role in his new movie as she had instructed? Or that I was staring at his muscles under his magenta shirt? Or was it because I had worn a pair of jeans that shamelessly revealed the shape of my derriere?

Amma's boomerang rattled me into immediate submission, turning back the clock to redeliver me into my foetal stage. Obviously, foetuses didn't understand that their entry into this world was through the dirty act of…And then suddenly another presence made her appearance: '*Stop it, Suchitra!*' she hissed.

Huh? How had Shrink entered Ramu's cabin now? Had she walked in with Amma too? I looked around suspiciously as Shrink's whiplash reverberated in my ears: '*You are just afraid of breaking your own conditioning. You've lost your confidence because of some recent setbacks. But I'm going to help you get out of that. It's my job.*'

Now, according to shrink protocol, shrinks are not *ever* supposed to do that, i.e., scold or talk down. I lost my cool. I yelled at her: 'Please don't use that sharp tone on me, Shrink. You know I am a classically trained singer and therefore my auditory canals are very finely tuned to even a fraction of a shift in tone. Even an eighth of a measure greatly affects pitch and timbre on the musical scale. Knowing how frayed my nerves already are, and that I feel like I'm on the verge of a nervous breakdown, the least you can do is show some sympathy...'

'Suchitra, are you okay?' This time the voice was Ramu's.

Huh? How did Ramu enter Shrink's cabin? Oh no, I hope he doesn't go tell the press that he saw me at a therapist's or something. I could do without another shameful scandal...

I collected my fragmenting mind. 'Of course I am, Ramu. Was just thinking why you would want to put up a grey and brown map of the world on your wall? It's so ugly. I could send you one of my bright colourful paintings you know, for some cheer...' *Damn oh damn – what had I just said? I was messing this up. Bad. Real bad.*

'I'm happy with my map,' Ramu said rather abruptly. 'Okay, forget about Shekhar. Tell me what are you up to these days?'

In spite of his placatory tone I sensed he was a bit offended. I needed to diffuse the situation without seeming too eager to please. But how? And then I began to wonder if Ramu was asking me about Shekhar because he was testing me to find out whether I had Shekhar's permission to marry him? Men are very territorial, you know – they respect and fear each other's power and don't have sex with other men's property. *Chheh Chheh! Sex, sex, sex. Shameless girl!* Don't get me wrong. I'm not a lecherous frustro out to trap innocent men like Ram Gopal

Varma under false pretences. It's just... just that...Besides, once we were married and had children, after socially and legally sanctioned sex, I could always teach him a little something about colour and dress sense and about hugs and ...

Stop getting distracted and disgusting, Chitty. Concentrate on the task at hand and get to the point. And that's an order! Slap! Whack! Dishoom!

'Erm...what did you say, Suchitra?'

'Huh? I didn't say anything, Ramu. Waiting for you to tell me...' *God, had he really heard me speak to myself? That too in Shrink's voice with its nasal twang?*

I quickly faked a sneeze – just in case Ramu had heard me talking aloud to myself. That way he would think I had a cold and that's why my voice sounded nasal. I wobbled my head theatrically. 'Oh god, this viral is making me delirious...' *Sidetracking subterfuge strategy – sure to succeed.*

'Uh...well...have you seen the film *Bitter Moon*?'

I was shocked. 'That *disgusting* one with all those sex scenes? Isn't that the one where the hero takes the heroine on a romantic holiday and escapes by abandoning her alone in a plane? Roman Polanski, right? The pervert was jailed for sodomizing a thirteen year old...'

Cough cough. (Oh how I love a man who clears his throat like that. Delicate yet masculine.)

'You see, what excited me in that film was the male–female dynamic. It just proved in such a simple way that men and women are so different...' Ramu continued in his trademark soft lilt.

'How did you see something that wasn't there, Ramu? How come I missed it? All I remember from that sick movie is when he asks her to pee on him for titillation and when he abandons her in the aircraft and runs away from commitment. Ramu, of course, didn't comment on the fact that I was mixing up the story lines of several movies in my dicordant haze. Staring flatly at me he allowed me to vent on, 'Why is the male–female dynamic so lopsided? Can it never work unless the woman agrees to junk her brains in the bin and be nothing but a servile sex slave?'

Dramatic pause from Ramu. Followed by an intense deep stare for a few seconds. Why was he playing these childish games? *'Yes' is a simple three-letter word, Ramu – so easy to pronounce. Even with a Telugu accent that makes it sound more like 'ess' with an E for Easter, instead of a 'Yes' with a Y for Yanking Off.*

'*Hmm*…interesting…' Longer pause. More intense staring for more seconds. Finally he spoke: 'Another film I'm planning is a one on office dynamics and how corporates function. The politics, romances, etc. Looking for some writers for it. What are you busy with these days, Suchitra?'

'Oh that's fab, Ramu. Have you heard of this book called *Office Politics*? By Sharon Lecherous or something...'

Oops! Did I just say 'Lecherous' instead of 'Gerlach'? Be like Queen Elizabeth the First – I scolded myself silently, drawing this time not from my own reserves but from the acting prowess of Cate Blanchet. After all, I had been there when Shekhar explained to Cate that the white mask that the Queen wore in the movie *Elizabeth* was but a metaphor for cunning and camouflage. Never reveal your true feelings. Keep 'em guessing, Sherlock. Now I intended doing just that.

'What a coincidence, Ramu,' I said, faux chirpily. 'I ordered the book on Amazon just last week. Great idea. Superb. Really superb. In fact, I would say brilliant. I'll bring it across to your office later.'

'No, no need for that...'

Oh-oh. Was that brief twitch in his eyes fleeting passion or frenzied panic?

'Well…'

'You asked me what I'm working on, right?'

Brainy and well-informed projection to impress potential husband was the call of the moment. 'Have you heard about the findings of the Stanford University survey, Ramu?'

OMG, I would kill Chandni for feeding my brain with this rubbish just as I was leaving.

'Well…' He waited for me to elaborate.

'Apparently,' I said, using my best, casually-well-informed voice, 'the folk at Stanford University interviewed half the world. And then by placing chips on, inside, and around people's skulls, wrists, thighs and buttocks to gauge the authenticity of the responses they received from the participants, they tried to study the relationship between stress and disease – and they arrived at these conclusions...They then fed this data into their computers; charting it scientifically with dots and squares and triangles and colour-coding so that its veracity was foolproof and would be accepted by the rest of the global scientific community as theory and not just random conjecture...'

'Random conjecture…*hmm*…interesting use of words...'

'You know what random conjecture is, right? Like that rubbish about the Ganesha idol drinking milk or the statue of Jesus Christ at Bandra Junction shedding a tear? Obviously, the global scientific community didn't believe *that*, even though thousands were eyewitness to these historical events. Where were the maps and diagrams? Einstein had to prove E=mc^2 the same way. Till he presented that theorem in noughts and crosses to explain speed and velocity, he too was considered mad. The same goes for Newton and the apple. So the Stanford guys did the same thing. I can bring the diagram across if you like along with the *Office Politics* book,' I offered, adding helpfully, 'You'll understand it better.'

'Uh...no, no. No need for that…' Ramu said hurriedly.

Dammit was I imagining the OMG WTF look in his eyes or was it my own low self-esteem and paranoia playing tricks on me? But time was short and there were few chances left. Sooner or later, I assured myself, it would all work out. And my wedding invite to Chandni and Sangita would be signed, sealed and delivered. So I bashed on regardless:

'So, basically, what this pathbreaking "leaning towards the spiritual but proven to be irrefutably scientific" Stanford University survey theory says is that – And here I quote verbatim, *haan* – Quote "Among other things, one of the best things a man can do for his health is to be married to a woman" Unquote. Did you know, Ramu, being with women actually helps create serotonin – a neurotransmitter that combats depression and creates a general feeling of well-being?'

'Suchitra, please excuse me, I have a meeting now. The person is waiting outside...'

My mind flew all over the place. *Oh god. Oh god. How do I make this work?* The ceiling was falling over my head again. The hum…the static…I struggled to disperse the fog in my brain and focus on his soft voice.

'Suchitra,' he was saying, 'let me be honest with you...'

'Of course, Ramu. I expect nothing else from the man who made *Satya*. It's why I'm here. We are very similar in that way...'

'Suchitra, I think you have misunderstood me. Completely. We are not similar at all. In fact, we are totally the opposite. I will *never* get married again. Never. I don't believe in the institution of marriage. I am just not the marrying kind. I use women only for sex and I'm very sure that's not what you want. I like women's bodies, not their brains. In my opinion a woman should be seen and not heard.'

OMG! What was I hearing? Help! Somebody help me. I'm getting very scared. Please come and save me. Please, Nana – hurry up. I'm feeling dizzy and disoriented. Where am I? Who am I? What's going on? Why does it feel like I'm asphyxiating? Answer me, Nana – you can't live your whole life in silence. Oh what's the use...I can't hear anything any more with all this rubble in my ears and nose... Help, Nana, help! Pleeeaase! Have you really gone deaf or are you just ignoring me?

'Don't feel bad, Suchitra. It's not that I don't like you. I think you're hot and most beautiful. But I am not the kind of person you need...'

I could taste the bile as it rose in my throat.

'I don't believe in marriage and commitment and I am sure that is what you are looking for. You'll have to excuse me – I have a person waiting for me outside. Sorry...'

OMG! That S word again. Why did it follow me everywhere however hard I tried to run away from it?

S for Southie.

S for Sex.

S for *Somebody Save Suchitra!*

I stumbled out in a daze. *Ouch!* my head. My heart. My brain. My muscles. My bones.

Why did everything hurt so much?

Contract! Freeze! Expand!

Crrraaacckk!

5

My saviour for the next few days, Indu the masseuse, flattened, kneaded and pummelled my post-mortem-like rigor mortis away, greatly inspired and encouraged by the thousand buck tips I thrust into her delighted palms. If the only road to kindness was money, I would happily go broke.

Sleep. A sweet sleep. Plenty of sleep. A long sleep. No phone calls, no meetings, no meditation, no homework. Just sleep. *Zzzzztttt!*

'*Didi, aap kitne acche ho. Sweeeeet. Sundar sundar. Koi nahin bol sakta hai ki aapki itni badi baby hai. Aap khud baby lagti ho. Aur aap ki kala. Wah wah! Kya acche painting banate hain aap. Sundar sundar candle banate hain. Mujhe ek candle do na, didi? Mujhe candle bahut acha lagta hai...*'

(Sister – you're so nice. Sw*ee*t. Pretty, pretty. Nobody can tell that you have a child this big; you look like such a baby yourself. And your art! What lovely paintings you make. Such fantastic candles too – give me one candle na, sister? I like candles ve*ry* much.)

I told her to take them all. I would make some more to keep myself busy when I did finally wake up from this long delirious sleep.

'*Aap itna rote kyon ho, didi? Aap jaisi khubsurat ladki ko duniya ki sabse khush ladki hona chahiye – jaise Shahrukh Khan kehta hai na, aapke picture* Kabhi Haan Kabhi Naan *mein?*

(Why do you cry so much, sister? A beautiful girl like you should be the happiest girl in the world – just like Shahrukh Khan says to you in your film *Kabhi Haan Kabhi Naan.*)

'*Didi, aap abhi picture kyon nahin karte?*'

(Why don't you act in films now?)

Why couldn't Indu the masseuse STFU? Because all I wanted was sleep! To just sleeeep. Forever and ever…oh no! I couldn't do that. Who'd look after Kaveri if I never woke up?

'*Mein nay suna aap kitaab bhi likhte hain? Wah, Didi, wah! Aap ke maathe par Saraswati baithi hain.*'

(I have heard you write books too? Amazing! Saraswati – the goddess of knowledge, resides in you.)

I gave Indu another thousand buck tip. Her hokum was drawing me out of my catatonia and that was a very good sign.

'*Didi, aap bura na maane toh mein ek baat, poochoon? Aap dubara shaadi kyon nahi kar lete? Aap kitneee achheee hain – kissi ko bhi khush rakh saktee hain...*'

(Sister, if you don't mind can I ask you one more thing? Why don't you get married again? You are *such* a nice girl – you could keep any man happy...')

Boooooo Hoooooo! Out! Get out! *Right* now! And I'm taking my tip back!

So what choice did I have other than to allow my girlies back into my life? Now that Ramu had refused to marry me, I had no one but my gal pals with whom to kill time. And if what the Stanford university survey said was true, it would eventually be good for my health and well-being. More so than body massages by simpering sycophants.

And so Sangita was back with me the next day. I watched

warily as she carefully scrutinized the Stanford map that Chandni had sent me

'OMG!' Sangita slapped her forehead, aghast. 'This is not the right map. No wonder you've messed this up so badly...'

'What do you mean, it's not the right map? It's what Chandni sent along with the survey...'

Sangita looked shocked. 'What you're looking at, dear Suchitra, is a map of a cat brain – incidentally also posted on the Stanford University website...'

Cat brain? *Cat* brain? Why would Chandni send me a map of a cat's brain, for god's sake? The *bitch*!

It was as if Sangita read my thoughts. 'No, she's not a bitch ya – just hopelessly dumb. The second part of the survey was about pets being good for people too – but only *after* girlfriends. They had put up all the maps together...'

'Huh? Was she serious?'

'You know Chandni – she's such a duffer. She obviously downloaded the wrong map!' Sangita pooh-poohed, rushing to my computer to download and print the right map as she carried on, explaining things in that patronizing, knowledgeable way of hers: 'In fact, even this particular "girlfriends are good for health" survey had two maps. One the actual and the other the interpretation...'

And then with a flourish, to the imagined sounds of a rising concerto, Sangita thrust the paper into my trembling palms, 'This, my dear, is the right map!'

Sangita's nose touched the fan. Even though she said nothing I could *hear* the standing ovation she was giving herself for this amazing revelation about the cat brain map that she had passed on to me, armed with which I had *completely* humiliated myself

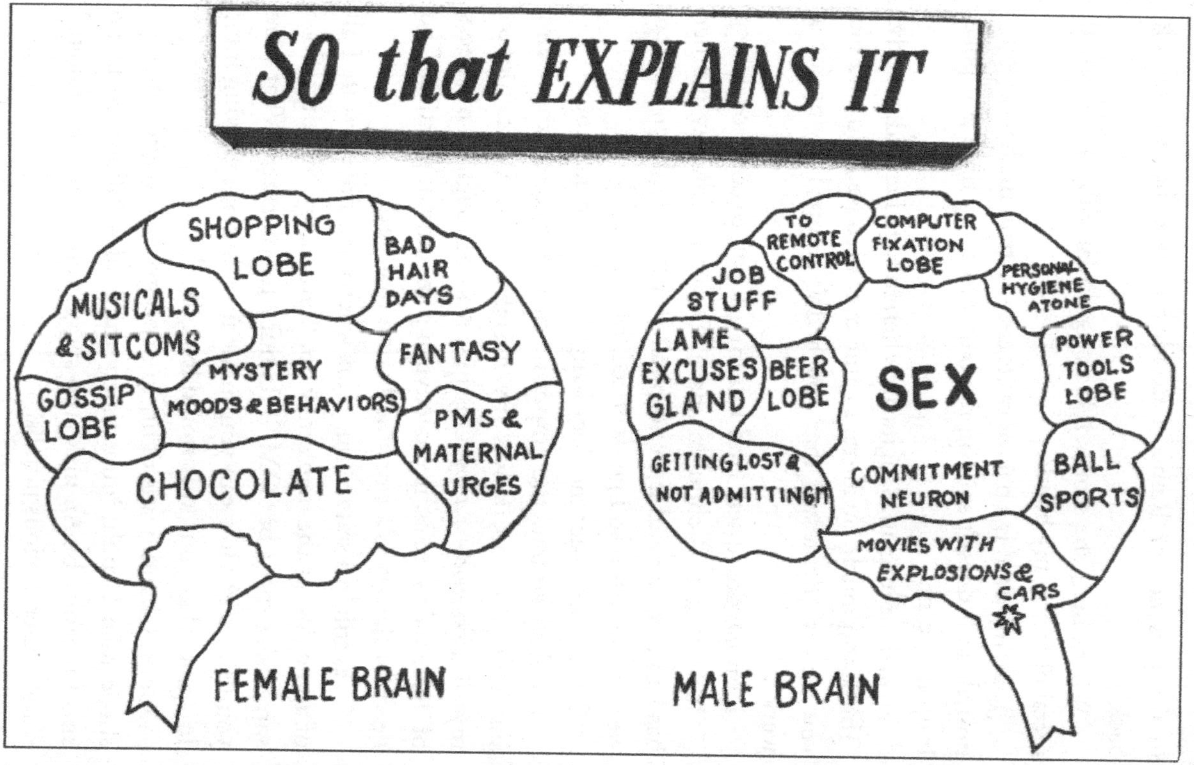
SO that EXPLAINS IT
SHOPPING LOBE
BAD HAIR DAYS
MUSICALS & SITCOMS
FANTASY
MYSTERY
MOODS & BEHAVIORS
GOSSIP LOBE
PMS & MATERNAL URGES
CHOCOLATE
FEMALE BRAIN
TO REMOTE CONTROL
COMPUTER FIXATION LOBE
JOB STUFF
PERSONAL HYGIENE ATONE
LAME EXCUSES GLAND
BEER LOBE
SEX
POWER TOOLS LOBE
GETTING LOST & NOT ADMITTING IT
COMMITMENT NEURON
BALL SPORTS
MOVIES WITH EXPLOSIONS & CARS
MALE BRAIN

in the presence of Ramu. I decided I owed her something back.

'What's that? she scorned, looking disdainfully at the small metal object in my hands.

'That, my dear, is a pair of tweezers – to trim the hair in your nostrils so it doesn't spill on to your chin every time you poke it up in the air.'

I had done it again. Sangita drew herself together, indignantly. 'This is too much, Suchitra. I came over because Indu told me you were so depressed that you hadn't stopped crying for a week...'

'I am *not* depressed. And I didn't ask you to come over.'

'It's my fault. I shouldn't have. Do you know my mother has had a stroke and is in hospital? But Indu said you've been weeping nonstop so I got worried. My mistake.'

Slam! Crash! – let the door bang! Sangita stormed out.

I looked around the empty room in a haze of anger and suspicion. No, no, it was my mistake. *Beware,* I cautioned myself. *Everybody is a spy*. Gossip spreads through all members of the female species, irrespective of proximity or position. The need for flattery is a worse addiction than sex!

I was still in a state of flummox when Chandni burst in. Full of apologies for the map screw up. 'I'm *so* sorry, Suchitra. So*oo* sorry. So*oo* sorry, but OMG! Ramu? Are you *crazy*? What were you thinking? How can you suddenly think of marrying him? Imagine what your kids would look like?'

Oops! Chandni was right. In my eagerness to grab the only single man I could immediately think of – influenced in no small measure by Amma's auto suggestion – I had overlooked some rather obvious pitfalls.

'But take it as a blessing, ya. Imagine if he had preyed on your vulnerability and used you just for sex. At least he was respectful of your needs, instead of just his own. One day you'll thank him. Listen I have an idea...'

After sending me a map of a cat brain instead of a human one, if she thought I was going to listen to her ever again she was even dumber than I gave her credit for: 'What now, Chandni? You want me to send Ramu some jojoba oil for his soft skin? Puhleeez. Give me a break!'

'No, no, don't be silly.' Chandni had another plan. A new one that would redeem my pitiful position in my own eyes and throw Ramu off-track too.

'Tell him you were doing research for a book on the male species and their reactions to marriage, or something. Make up some clever theory. And send him the books as promised so he knows you haven't taken any of this seriously *at all* but were instead just *testing* him. But not the maps, *haan*...then he may get suspicious...'

'Oh shut up!'

So Chandni promised to deliver the books, personally, the next day. In return for this though, she too wanted a favour – I had to accompany her to a party that very night and she wouldn't take no for an answer. It was the launch of Dior in India. High-glitz, glamour, and gossip.

'But what will I wear? Nothing's going to fit...' I said morosely as I contemplated pulling down a curtain under which to hide my 'bloated-with-depressed-bingeing' body.

'Don't be stupid. You look just fine and you haven't put on any weight. It's all in your head '

Of course it's all only in our head, girlfriend. Which part of life isn't?

'Listen, just come. I insist. Start meeting people – work. You're so talented, don't waste it.'

Yes, but who the hell wanted to work? I wanted to marry and have babies. Period. And the acting work I was being offered these days was just appalling. Samosa-making aunty with a twenty-five-year-old son! Can you imagine? How dare they offer me something like that? Did I look like I could be the mother of a twenty-five-year-old? Wasn't it bad enough that I had started to be called aunty at the age of twenty-five by thirty-five year olds who didn't know how else to address Shekhar Uncle's wife?

'You should be happy that you are in people's radar at all, considering you don't do anything to seek work. Instead you just keep refusing everything that comes your way,' Amma had scolded when I'd complained.

But how could I not? Refuse, that is? Imagine, the only other offer I'd had since the samosa one was one in which the movie producer told me they needed a *very* powerful actress. Somebody with a *very strong* presence – 'This role will turn you into a female Amrish Puri, madam!'

Out! *Out!* My life is hard enough without being insulted further.

'Okay forget work – it will cheer you up if nothing else. How long are you going to stay locked indoors?'

Chandni persisted, until I had no choice but to relent.

♋

The plan was to go dancing at the newly-opened nightclub 'Z bar' immediately after the launch. Sangita would join us directly there from work because she never attended these page

3 parties – said they were too dumb. Too-dumb, my ass. Next time, I would tell her the truth about that too. She just got a complex being around glamorous people. 'They are not dumb, girlfriend. You're just ugly...' ha ha.

Actually I was quite surprised Sangita had agreed to come clubbing after the tweezer incident. Simpering Chandni I could handle, but sourdough Sangita tonight, maybe not. But, then again, since my future husband might just be at that party tonight...*hmm.* I was hopeful there was a chance that I could be dancing at my own wedding before the night was over and then I could put Ramu in that room too.

You know, the one I intended to set ablaze along with my girlfriends, Amma and Shrink...

6

We seated ourselves in Chandni's brand-new BMW presented to her by her ooh-*sooo*-loving husband. We were on our way to the Dior launch and had stopped outside Ramu's office en route – just three blocks from my own apartment – to drop off the copy of *Office Politics* that I had promised him. Why wait till tomorrow to redeem my dignity? The fresh smell of the fancy leather cushions in the car was making me nauseous.

'Look, I'm not doing it to show off or anything,' Chandni pleaded. 'Sanjit gifted it to me just yesterday so...'

'Of course you're showing off, dumbo. Just you wait till...'

Wait a minute. Who were all these uniformed, gun-toting men crawling outside Ramu's office? No wonder he had been so uptight with me that day. He should have just told me that Dawood or Chota Shakeel or Rajan or Munna – or whoever the current (in)famous gangster was – had issued him a death warrant. I would have backed off and saved my marriage proposal for another day. But men are so inhibited when it comes to expressing their emotions, *na*? I had been selfishly thinking just of myself instead of trying to understand him better. The fact that he had given me time of day even under such perilous circumstances proved to me once again that he was a good man after all. I had to help him.

Since we were not permitted to enter the office premises we cornered an assistant as he was leaving the office, stepping out on to the road. I poked my head out of the window. 'Hey,

Thani! What are all these cops doing outside Ramu's office? Is he under some underworld threat or something?'

He crouched down by my window and whispered, 'Those are not cops. They are bodyguards from a private security company. Apparently, some psycho chick has been stalking Ramu and trying to convince him to marry her. You know how he is, *na*? I've never seen him so scared even of Dawood and Chota Rajan, as he is of this psycho chick.'

The feeling of nausea rammed into me again. *Oh god! Oh god, please...Please don't humiliate me anymore. Please, please please...*

'Did he say who this chick was?'

'No, don't know her name. But apparently she stays somewhere in the neighbourhood. So he's shit scared that she can just walk over anytime with her marriage proposal again.'

Thank god for the champagne in Chandni's brand-new BMW's booze compartment.

'Can you imagine the debauchery of having a compartment for alcohol in a car? That too in a country like India where you drive by people who can't even afford a single meal a day!' I said, putting up a brave front, trying to keep my face from crumpling into a waterfall of tears.

'I agree, it's terrible. Completely elitist. We'll discuss it later. Right now just have this champagne and enjoy yourself,' Chandni said, coaxing a glass of bubbly gently into my shaking hands, pretending she didn't notice my tears even as she handed me the tissue, apologizing over and over for the cat brain map that she had mistakenly sent me. 'If only I had given you the right map in the first instance...' she said as we drew up to the gates of the Dior event.

But my mind had glazed. I couldn't hear anything any more. The static was back, humming through my brain as I staggered down the red carpet at the Dior party trying hard to conceal my paunch and swollen eyes from the paparazzi.

When one photographer insisted I pose next to a skinny model, I showed him my middle finger. Would rather have *that* appear in the papers than a picture of me standing next to Miss Pencil Stick, looking like a bazooka blimp, arms the size of a banyan tree trunk.

I picked up a glass of wine in each hand and mingled. Even though I couldn't really see much any more. *La di dah da dah – la di dah.* Clink! Click! Circulate! *Muah! Muah! Muuuuaaaaah!*

Aaah! There was Karan Johar – standing in the corner with his 'I'm-so-intensely-clever' expression. Hey, he's single! Why hadn't I thought of *him* before? So what if there could never be *Kuch Kuch Hota Hai* between us? I could live with *Dostana.* And wasn't *Kabhi Khushi Kabhi Gham* life's mantra anyway? I ignored Chandni tugging at my sleeve and tried my best to lose her in the crowd as I ambled over to Karan, taking another large gulp of wine for fortification.

'Hey, Karan. Would you like to make your mother happy?'

'Hi Suchitra. How are you doing?'

'Listen, you haven't answered my question. But, anyway, why don't you marry me, Karan, and make your mother happy?'

'My mother's already very happy. And why on earth would you want to get married again?'

'Because I just want a rich, powerful man to look after me.'

'Me too – ha ha.'

Ha ha – get lost! I'm gonna put you in that burning room too with my girlies and my shrink and Amma and Ramu and...

'Suchi baby – how are you and why do you have two glasses of wine in your hands?' That was Ken Ghosh. He plucked the wine glasses from my hand and placed them aside, thrusting a glass of water in their place. I swayed and sighed. He was married – and so of no use to my ambitions to be a bride.

'No, no Ken – one glass is for my friend. I'm just holding it for her till she gets back. Have you seen her? Short, petite… you've met her ya, at many parties at my place...'

'Suchi, you're okay *na*, baby?' Ken had always treated me like a kid – sexless, a eunuch even. Can you imagine, when we were shooting my *Jabse Dekha* (Ever Since I Saw You) music video – and this was in my pop superstar days in the late nineties when I used to get fan mail in blood and had little kids calling themselves Suchitra – Ken had had the gall to stall shooting till I changed my cleavage-revealing outfit into something more suitable. 'Suchi baby – a face like yours cannot have a cleavage.'

'Well it does now – so deal with it,' I had snapped. He was sounding like Amma and it was pissing me off big time! My video, my song, *my* wish – what was *his* problem?

But Ken had not relented. There had been a three-hour embargo on the sets. I didn't change; he didn't shoot. Finally, the music company had to intervene and so we arrived at a compromise. I faced the camera in the same red cleavage-revealing dress, but Ken made me stand at an angle with my shoulders to the camera and shot only tight close-ups of my face!

But all that was a thing of the past. Today I would show him that I was all grown up and determined to have my way. I decided to play it straight: 'Ken – do you have any friends who would like to marry me?'

'You know my friends, ya Suchi – they are all like me. We only like loose and immoral women.' Big kiss on the forehead, another glass of water. 'How are you going home? You have a car? You want my driver to drop you? He can drop you now and come back to fetch me, not a problem.'

Of course it's a problem you bloody lover of loose immoral women, refusing to find me a husband. You gonna be in that burning room too…sooon. As soon as I get…

Oh dear, the room was spinning. The static in my ears had crescendoed to a roar. The ceiling was inching closer and closer to the floor. *Ouch!* My head. I couldn't stand any more. I stepped out of my 5-inch heels and held them in my left hand while grabbing another glass of wine from a passing waiter. Where was Chandni? I tried calling her mobile – she obviously couldn't hear it over the din of chatter. Should I find Ken and ask him to get his driver to take me home?

As I stumbled about I bumped headlong into Nagesh Kukunoor – *Whoa!* He was single, Telugu, *and* had an engineering degree from America. Plus, he was my neighbour too – our windows looked into each other's. Wow! Perfect! Amma would be thrilled with my choice. I couldn't believe I hadn't thought of him before – dumb, dumb, *dumb*. Just like Chandni. Where the hell was she? I prayed she wouldn't show up right in the middle of my marriage proposal to Nagesh.

I sidled up to Nagesh and struck a pose. No, no, Suchitra, a voice in my head advised, try another angle. With the newly gained knowledge that men liked loose, immoral women only for sex, I needed to show some ingenuity. What good were my brilliant academic genes if I couldn't use them at the right moment? Be an inventor, not a historian, Chitty. That way,' you and Amma can both still have your way and the sterling values of the Indian middle-class will not be tainted.

But how could I do that without coming across as a born-again sex maniac? No, no, I needed to keep it subtle. Apply some reverse sexual psychology and see if he would bite the bait.

'Hey, Nagesh,' I grabbed another glass of wine and undulated seductively. 'Why don't you come to your window tomorrow morning and do an *angdaee*?'

'What's an "angdaee"?'

That's one thing about these Southie guys who have grown up outside of Mumbai. They never ever learn Hindi – even though they make movies in the language.

'Arrey – *angdaee,* ya Nagesh. You know, stretch – *strreeetchhh.* Like the old Hindi film heroines did to attract the hero. They would come to their windows and stretch their arms over their heads languorously. And at the exact moment that their chest was most pointed and thrust forward, a gust of wind would blow the heroine's dupatta away, exposing her boobies. And the hero would get all horny and…' *You want loose and immoral baby – I'm gonna give you just that.*

'Oh man! Suchitra. My shoes have just caught fire. Gotta run. Have you met Siddharth?' Nagesh hurriedly thrust the first man available in front of me and beat a hasty retreat.

Ooooh! Who was *this* sweet-dish? God please make him single – please.

And yes, please run, Nagesh. Because the room I'm going to set ablaze is in your house.

Now since Siddharth had overheard my *angdaee* proposal to Nagesh and I was too intelligent to try the same tactic again, I asked him: 'You have children?' After all, can't ask a strange directly if he's married, *na*? That would be a bit…but never mind. Once I had taken Siddharth home tonight and had sex with him (since men like loose and immoral women only for sex) I would gag his mouth, tie him to the bed, and call the priest to quickly perform the marriage ceremony.

'Yes, two. In fact my wife was in school with you...'

Dang! There goes my husband. 'Really?'

'Yeah, Monica.'

OMG! not good old '*chaddi choomchee*' whom Amma had banned for coming home in shorts and showing her arse.

This earth was too small for me – I'm Pluto bound.

'Monica. Wow. Monica – what's she doing now?

'She's a housewife.'

'Oh, just like me. Housewives are best you know, for looking after home and children.'

'What are you busy with these days? Not singing? I was a ig fan of that song of yours "*Dum Tara*". And Monica keeps 'king about that song you used to sing in school, "*Nobody's ild*", and how it made your principal cry...'

Hello? So what was I supposed to sing now? *Nobody's Wife?*

not singing these days. Not really. I just don't seem to get me. And you? What do you do?'

1 a politician.'

s approaching outer space rapidly; my rocket about to 1on all would be well.

olitics, huh? *Kewl!* Do you know Rahul Gandhi?'

om zoomed. Sweet-dish Siddharth, husband of *chaddi*

Monica laughed. I needed to get home before I I bent down to put my shoes on and fell to the shing my head against the table.

'OMG – are you okay? Do you need some help?'

'Ya, I do. I need to know if you know Rahul Gandhi. He's still single, right? Can you ask *him* if he'd like to marry me?' I tried desperately to prop myself up on my elbow and dimple sweetly.

Chandni arrived at the precise moment I fainted.

PART II

Nucking Futs!
A Parable of Phobias, Manias and Other Assorted Nervous Disorders

7

'You will *not* have a nervous breakdown. It's my job to ensure you don't. I'm sorry about what happened. It's not your fault...'

What bloody sorry? Shrink didn't look sorry at all – her face the same neutral deadpan as always. How could she think she was deceiving me for even a second? Just because she was a doctor? Couldn't she tell that my nervous breakdown was not in the future tense but in the present-continuous? I was thick in the throes of one already. Shrink's shallow assurance was no doubt just a devilish ploy to ensure I remained forever dependent on her and that she kept getting richer and richer.

Today she had arrived in a Mercedes.

Purchased from my hard-earned alimony.

A few years from now it would be a Rolls Royce – from the same source.

Did she think I was such a fool?

'Of course you are not a fool. In fact, quite the opposite. Sometimes that's what makes it all the more confusing; because emotion and intelligence are two different words.'

'Thanks for telling me they are two different words. I'm a writer, you know, with two published books already.'

'Yes, I know that, Suchitra. And I'm explaining it to you because I know you'll understand. Thing is, basically, we have to use our intelligence to understand emotion.'

Oh no – I didn't understand anything.

Nothing at all. Not anymore. Never did, actually.

There was no past, present, or present-continuous tense for this 'I-don't-understand-anything-at-all' dilemma. To which the road ahead loomed even more tense – tenser, tensest – than ever. And it looked bloody bleak in the far, further and furtherest future-continuous.

My head started to spin painfully. For the first time in my life I actually wished I had been truly and completely hare-brained. Like Chandni. So that my skull wouldn't try to crack open with the effort of trying to find a way out of this labyrinthine maze.

Oh god! I pleaded with the powers that be, in my next life please make me an amoeba!

I returned home from this pointless, 'waste-of-my-hard-earned-alimony' visit to Shrink, to some more nasty news. My parents were arriving early the next morning. Oh dear god! The thought of Amma's disapproval of my tripe made my intestines gripe. I needed to calm and arm myself but how? I spent another restless sleepless night, preparing my defence. Stopping only at 7.00 in the morning to walk the dogs. When I got back, there they were, waiting for me.

♋

'It's my previous life's karma that I have had to live to see this day! What did I do wrong that you have turned out like this? You have become totally shameless!' Amma paced at the door clutching her forehead dramatically.

'Previous life's karma? How about *this* life, Amma? How about owning up to your flaws instead of constantly pointing out mine? And, besides, I was just following your instructions and behaving like a prostitute – as actresses are *supposed* to behave, right?'

'*Aiyyo* – do something, Nana. What has happened to our Chittu? Why is she behaving like this?'

Aah – there was my father, further down the hall, flashing me his trademark hapless smile. I ignored him and turned back to face my mother. 'Nothing has happened to me, Ma. Just leave me alone.'

'What leave you alone? So that you drop down drunk at public functions or marry that Iqbal and start slaughtering goats in Kaveri's presence? I have come here for her sake, not yours.'

Amma and Nana had booked their ticket from Bangalore to Mumbai the minute they had seen the photograph in the papers. The sensational one, taken at that exact moment in the Dior party when I fell to the ground and crashed my head. I had only a fuzzy memory of it, though. And, tragically, no recall of what had ensued immediately after. Just my luck. No memory of when, apparently, sweet-dish Sidharth had carried me, totally inebriated and unconscious, in his arms to the car – requesting and bribing a few photographers to refrain from clicking pictures. Not for my sake – but *his*.

Still.

Dang! If only if I had stayed cognizant a little while longer. Aaah....to *actually* savour the delight of being swept off the ground and lifted into a man's strong arms! How much more fulfilling that would be than the cursory hug with a non-breasted body, which was my lot these days.

Still, I thought, Amma had given me a great idea once again...I decided that the next time I Scrabbled with Pankaj I would pretend to break my toe under the table just before the game finished. And then I would scream and pretend to be in so much pain that he would have no choice but to sweep me into his arms and carry me to my bed. I would, of course, insist he leave as soon as he laid me down flat, just as our cheeks brushed ever so lightly, and our arms reluctantly disentwined. It was imperative he go at precisely that moment and not even a few seconds later because I couldn't have him examining my foot for injury and calling my bluff, now could I? *Oooooh! Yum yum yum.* I could feel the flush creep into my cheeks.

Amma glowered at me. I quickly averted my flushed cheeks, and made a big show of wiping my face. 'This colour of blush-on is too bright a pink, don't you think?'

'It's 7.30 in the morning. Do you always walk the dogs with make-up on?' Amma squinted hard at me.

'Next time I'll remember to try Mac,' I declared rubbing my cheeks vigorously. '*Such* a pity that Indian products have become so substandard – the colour takes forever to wipe off.'

The real pity of course, was that I had zero-recall of asking sweet-dish to leave the immoral, scandalously attired, *chaddi choomchee* Monica and marry me instead. Now *that* would have been something, wouldn't it? i.e. if he had agreed? It would have spared me the anxiety of scheming and executing my next 'sweep-me-off-my-feet-and-take-me-to-bed' plan.

I forced myself to focus on the present. Amma, it seemed, was convinced I was possessed by some form of alcohol-induced dementia. She fixed me with her most disapproving look.

'No, Amma. I *don't* have a drinking problem. Don't worry so much. That incident was a one-off – a Mania Potu.'

'Don't try to use big words to distract from the issue. Try those stunts with your daddy. I am not easily impressed,' Amma snorted.

Truth be told, Amma has always had a bit of a complex about her limited knowledge of big English words, having studied in a Tamil medium school and all. That is why, when we were growing up, she had harped on other aspects – like 'Get your figure of speech right' or 'I'm a teacher, ra kanna, and I know everything'. She would often confuse words too, like the time when I had caused the kitchen to flood, age eleven.

This unfortunate incident had happened because I hadn't closed the tap to the right like she had instructed, turning the knob to the left instead. If she had said it kindly I may have considered obeying her for a change, but the bark of her command had forced me to do just the opposite. Left or right – really, what difference did it make? A tap's a tap, right?

And a slap's a slap too – *Ouch!* 'Why are you always so disobedient? Why do you have to *contribute* everything I say?'

A slap hurts a lot too, Amma, and not just the cheek. It breaks one's heart in half and folds it into a teardrop.

And contribute to what? If Amma had asked me to contribute to cleaning up the mess I would have done so quietly – but she hadn't. And therefore, I didn't. How was that my fault? Nana, the word wizard, had apologized and explained, 'Sorry, ra kanna. She mixed up the words. She meant *contradict*...'

But that only threw me further. 'So *I* get slapped because *she* makes a mistake?'

Nana had perfected the 'If you can't convince Chittu – confuse her' maxim. 'She is very tired, that's all. Had to take three extra lectures today on the Contribution of the British

Raj to the Development of the Indian Education System – so I think she mixed up the words *contradict* and *contribute*...'

And you don't think that's wrong, Nana? Amma should have been the one apologizing, not him. Nana's lack of concern, his apathy, had hurt more than Amma's slap – the teardrop would soon dry, but what about the stain it was leaving on my heart?

Of course, at that tender age I had not read the revelations of the Stanford University survey and so had been sadly clueless. How was I, with my stunted emotional development, to be able to possibly understand how inhibited men actually were when it came to expressing emotion?

Jobs? Yes.

Fishing? Yes.

But their feelings? No way!

It's the way god had made them – god's fault. Nothing to do with my daddy dearest.

And now that I was a grown up woman, enlightened by the findings of this remarkable, breakthrough survey, it was only mature and correct that I show some compassion and forgive Nana, for all the right, wrong and imagined follies committed against me.

I looked at my father. Since Nana was a man of few words – chosen carefully and painstakingly – it was important that I did that too. Choose my words carefully and painstakingly, that is. Just the way he had taught me to, in all the word games we had played through my childhood. How else could I prove that I was still daddy's precious girl – the most special child god had ever created – and bug Amma even more?

And how else could I remind myself that there *were* a few

things in life where I still stood a chance of success, after the abysmal failure of my marriage proposals?

Sadly, since my befuddled brain, in its current incoherent state, was incapable of conjuring up any words at all – leave alone longwinded, many-lettered ones, other than 'sex' and 'hugs' and 'murder', which would do me no good in proving to my upright, righteous parents that I was a good girl, I was – I had Googled words like 'inebriated', 'drunk', etc., the minute I knew they were going to arrive.

I mean, who uses real dictionaries, anymore? I even researched synonyms and antonyms and wrote them all down in my diary. Can't afford to make any mistakes and jumble up the words, *na*? I learnt these words and phrases by heart too, so I had them on tap and they poured off my lips without hesitation at the appropriate moment. I hoped Nana would be impressed – like when he used to pat me on the back and praise me to the skies when we played that 'What's the New Word Today' game.

Pleasing Amma wasn't going to be that easy but I would take one step at a time. Success, like happiness, was waiting for me at the end of this sharp U turn.

'Of course I know you're not easily impressed, Amma. With your level of accomplishment how can I *dare* even aspire to that? I am just telling you my diagnosis. My shrink says what I have is something different. Even more serious than "Mania Potu".'

I put on my best puppy dog expression, the one which when translated into Human Speak, said: 'I'm your helpless slave – only you, oh great mighty one, can save me,'; my experience as an actress once again coming to the fore; a facial expression perfected during the time of my marriage to a globally-renowned film director. I had learnt a few of these world-class nuances from observing his actresses on the set, the rest were my own guile. It worked – hell, it always did.

'*Aiyyo* – what, ra kanna?'

'It's called Dementia Pugilistica, Ma. Often mistakenly thought by laymen to be induced by alcohol because, physically, the patient appears drunk all the time even without touching a drop of liquor. It's quite a serious condition, this "Punch-Drunk Syndrome".'

I reined in my thoughts and tried to stay focused on my mother. Amma gazed hard at me, pursing her lips and narrowing her eyes. I attempted to squeeze out a tear – 'Please promise me you'll help me get rid of this disease,' I pleaded.

Begging and prostrating before elders has always got me what I wanted. It was only assertiveness – often mistaken for arrogance – that backfired and shot pellets straight into my skull. How long would I keep trying to pull them out? Some of them were too deeply embedded. Faking humility was the only path to atonement now – I gave it my all and squeezed a little more helplessness into my eyes

'Of course we will help you, ra kanna. That's why we are here. I will talk to Sudhakar about it.'

'No, no,' I protested quickly. 'This kind of dementia does not respond to allopathic drugs. It requires a different kind of treatment...'

'Why? Like what? Whatever it is we will get it for you. Don't worry, darling.'

'I don't know the name of the cure. But it's *very* important to leave the patient alone. *All* By Herself.'

'Alone, aa? Why? Is it contagious?'

'No, not contagious, just very dangerous to those around; more than to the patient herself. Because of the irrational mood swings, caused by the brain being squeezed to shut down, due to lack of oxygen...' I rambled on desperately.

'Oh my god! How did this Dementia or Punch-Drunk Syndrome or whatever it's called happen, ra kanna?'

'Dementia Pugilistica – that's the name. Here, I've written the spelling down for you.' I handed the piece of paper to Amma and asked Nana to take a look too. 'Not only is it called Punch-Drunk Syndrome, it's also called Boxer's Syndrome. You know why? Because it's a neurological disorder that affects mainly boxers who receive multiple blows on their head over a period of time.'

Now my parents looked big-time worried. 'You are not a boxer – it's impossible. We will talk to Sudhakar.'

'No, no, please don't bother him, because I think he is also suffering from the same disease. He too needs to be left alone.'

'How did this happen, ra kanna? Why are all my children suffering so much? After all the sacrifices I have made to see them happy and successful. What is this Boxer's Syndrome disease? How did both of you get it at the same time without having any interest in boxing or any other sport?'

'That's exactly what worried me, Ma. So I asked Sigmund Freud. And *he* explained that one doesn't necessarily get Boxer's Syndrome only from sparring in a boxing ring. Nagging and scolding and an "I'll-bash-you-on-the-head-if-you-don't-obey me" attitude from Ammas and Nanas is also a precipitating factor.'

'*Chheh! Kharmon!* Stop this nonsense!' Amma cried, distressed at my mocking.

But I just got more irascible. 'Why should I stop it? You better stop it and show some respect before your contradictory contributions make my disease fatal – understood?'

'Shut up,' Amma's look turned from concern to indignation. 'I am here for Kaveri. Not for you.'

Really? No shit, Sherlock. 'And you know what *else* Sigmund Freud told me? He said your mother is suffering from a Narcissistic Personality Disorder. That's why you always feel a sense of entitlement to being treated as superior. And assume that everybody has to defer to your wishes.'

Looking at my mother, I had often wondered why I had made it to the movies and not her – being the famous village beauty and all. Compliments from relatives had never been without the qualifying adage, 'But you are not a patch on your mother.' Or, 'You should have seen how beautiful your mother was when she was your age.' How did I care about any of that? I only wondered why everyone was so eager to please her and bow to her orders. Perhaps that's why the vapid world of the movies bored me so much – I had no patience for the vain, narcissistic delusions of the movie-star/mogul brigade. Oh Amma should have been in the movies for sure. I mean, Hitler was a failed artist too.

Amma was beginning to get deeply agitated. '*Aiyyo,* Nana, do something. What is wrong with our Chittu? What has happened to her? When will you grow up, ra Chitappa? You are too old to go on blaming everybody else for your unhappiness. Do you really feel I am like Hitler, then what about your daddy? If I started telling you things about him…*Aiyyo*…do something, Nana...'

'See, typical female Narcissistic Personality Syndrome – getting the male to do your distorted bidding,' I grinned, half hoping he would intervene. But what could Nana do? What had he ever done?

Sigmund Freud had explained that too: 'Nana has an Ostrich Personality Disorder. It's characterized by burying your head in the sand and lying low till the problem passes away...'

'I know you are very sad, ra kanna – but this amateur psychology is stupid and not helping you in any way. If only you had listened to me and married someone from your peer group like Venkatesh, and not somebody like Shekhar, you would not have such an inferiority complex. When will you learn to start using your time in a better way? That's why we have come – to help you.'

Great! Act as if you care and undermine and insult me at the same time all over again.

'I thought you had come only for Kaveri and not for me...'

'There is no difference between a mother and child. So you better learn to behave yourself before she picks up all your bad habits, understood?'

Crash! Boom! Bang! I had failed at faking humility too.

I immediately reverted to feeling like a helpless inverted foetus all over again. Alas , O lord! Prithee, where art thou?

In case you're wondering why my language has suddenly tipped to the archaic, it's because Shakespeare had been a big hit with Nana too. Along with the other great modern English classics in my growing up years. I used to nod my head in wonder every time he read out a passage from *Macbeth, Hamlet* or *A Midsummer Night's Dream.* Too scared to admit that I didn't understand a word:

Be advised, fair maid:
To you your father should be as a god,

One that composed your beauties, yea, and one
To whom you are but as a form in wax,
By him imprinted and within his power
To leave the figure or disfigure it.

Huh? What on earth was that? And how could I trust Shakespeare, *haan*? What if he was a trickster and mixed up words just like Amma? After all, Amma had written books too: *Education and Empowerment of Women in the British Raj* and *The Opium Trail and its Impact on Society*'. How could she falsely accuse me of being a shameless junkie and then conduct intensive research on how opium and other Celine Dion kinda drugs made the land rich? What sort of an oxymoron was that – a *contradiction* or a *contribution*? As if money is everything. Even gangsters and prostitutes have that, Amma would always contend. What mattered was AEIOU:

A – ACADEMICS and
E – ELDERS' GLORIFICATION
I – IMPOSED by
O – OBEDIENCE to
U – ULTIMATUMS.

'Because you cannot make a single word without a vowel – understood?'

'What rubbish, Amma! There are many words that don't contain vowels – cry, nymph rhythm, gypsy…'

'*Aiyyo*, Chitappa, stop being so frivolous all the time. Where is the character in these words? Has a gypsy or a nymph ever made it into history books? Think why?'

'"Why" is also a word without a vowel by the way,' I had shot back, but Amma wasn't listening to me any more…

Hmm... Maybe Amma did have a point on that one. Amma's AEIOU philosophy – deep buried and suppressed over many years of ensuing defiance and disorientation – had rushed into my mind on one of my especially incoherent days not so long ago.

That day the dark circles under my eyes were drooping to my toes and the puffiness around my eyes made them bulge beyond my nose. I was desperate to buy that expensive insomnia oil. Desperate was putting it mildly. I was at the end of my tether, really. I even tried the piles cream that a model friend of mine in London had suggested to reduce under-eye swelling, but to no avail. It was useless.

So with few choices left, in a last-ditch attempt, I decided to give Amma's AEIOU funda a chance. I sent my essential oil supplier a handwritten, autographed poem (on scented paper borrowed from Chandni, no less) instead of a cheque. Now this was quite a famous poem of mine, for god's sake, having already appeared in some papers and in a book called *A Clear Blue Sky* alongside Narayana Murthy and Ruskin Bond and other distinguished Indian writers. Didn't that amount to something?

Unfortunately, the ignoramus oil merchant obviously wasn't impressed. At all. He flatly refused to accept my payment in poetry and totally refused to part with the insomnia oil. 'Why are you not acting in films any more?' he asked pointedly instead.

Why did everybody always ask me that question? How was it any of their business?

'See, my daughter is a great fan of Shahrukh Khan. So if you can take her to meet him and get an autograph...then I will consider giving you the oil till you...' the oleaginous guy offered.

Preposterous! Glamour-struck bloody bozo! I told him I didn't want the oil in that case and asked him to return my autographed poem on scented paper immediately. Now the bugger refuses to answer my phonecalls. With the result that I have been forced to find another essential oil supplier. Who charges twice as much!

'Yes, Amma, yes. I bow down and salute you. A-E-I-O-U too – one tight slap!

'Aiyyo!'

Exactly what I said, Ma. But this one's in an anglicized twang – dig? That's how they say *Aiyyo* in London!

Uncanny that AEIOU pronounced with a western twang did indeed sound a lot like Kaveri's favourite word – *Aaeeww!* – or Gross! Only, unlike Amma, who used her *Aiyyos* in every line, Kaveri used it more discerningly. Like every time I placed a bowl of beans or carrots on the table and she went, '*Aaeeww!* Mamma, gross! Can't I have Maggi noodles instead?'

The last time she had asked that, I had clamped my hand down hard on Kaveri's mouth in panic. So as to not let Amma hear my daughter demand nutritionally-deprived food, that I, being the inadequate mother and all, was wrongly encouraging. It had made Kaveri cry in shock. I burst out crying too.

'I'm sorry, my baby. I didn't mean to do that. I just thought if Amma hears you asking for Maggi noodles she'll take off on me again and I just got scared and...' Gosh! I *was* cracking up!

'It's okay, Mamma. It didn't hurt me. I just got scared – you've never done something like that before.'

I hugged my baby tight – she held on to me fiercely.

8

Chandni came by a few days later and suggested I attend one of her kitty parties to lift my spirits.

No way, girlfriend.

I'm a Southie. It's less dishonorable for me to run naked on the beach and have sex with a total stranger than attend a *kitty* party. Even talking about a UFO sighting or talking to aliens would be more acceptable. That would at least give my folks hope that a great scientific discovery was around the corner. And the *Aiyyo*/AEIOU flag would soar high again, instead of sweeping the floor, in the way that attending a kitty party would surely assure.

Because a UFO sighting might still give my parents and assorted relatives the dim expectation that my brain cells had not completely died and putrefied – they were just a little warped; a temporary malfunction.

Like in the case of Subu Mama (an uncle of mine who some in the family believed was a reincarnation of Ramanujan – the world's greatest mathematician!) who spent the last few years of his life hiding behind tables and cupboards and doors, covering himself in burqas every time he left his house, convinced that NASA was after him to steal his brilliant 'never-thought-of-before' scientific formula. A path-breaking device for the sustainable illumination of planet earth. Aided by its finest natural resource, namely – the Great South Indian

Coconut. This gizmo he named CostraSubu – an abbreviation of Coconut Strand Solar Bulb. The last 'SO' from solar, of course, being replaced by 'SU' – the first two alphabets of Subu Mama's own first name, Subramanium.

Hell, if that Bengali chap Bose could do it why not him, Subu Mama reasoned. He was at least modest enough not to give it his name directly and call it the 'Subramanium Bulb' or some such vain appellation. And so CostraSubu it was.

The family never acknowledged Subu Mama's dementia – they just felt really sorry that his new solar light bulb invention using coconut strand had been rejected by the ASI – American Society of Inventors.

'Poor chap, Subu was just way ahead of his time,' they clucked disconsolately.

My mind flash-forwarded back from the CostraSubu coconut strand bulb incident to my almond-complexioned friend. 'So my lovely, you get the point, don't you? *Chitty can't kitty*. Sorry about that.'

'No, *I'm* sorry ya, it's because I keep talking about sex that you're reminded of it so much, *na*?' Chandni apologized. 'I didn't realize it was causing you so much pain. So forget kitty parties and sex – I'm sure some good old retail therapy will get rid of that hum in your head.'

I looked at her, aghast. Was she crazy? Her daily shopping allowance was equivalent to Kenya's GDP, if not more. And even if I got over that complex how could I deal with her dress size? She was thin, thin, thin…4 whole sizes smaller than me.

Uff! Some girls have all the luck.

Then Sangita, who dropped by later, said I needed to take a firm stand if I wanted to sort out the blues and I had to ask Amma to do two things. Right away:

1. To stop nagging me once and for all, and if that didn't work ...
2. To leave.

But how could I ask her to leave? 'Are you mad? She's my mom, ya. And my parents have only come because I told them I can't bear to be alone any more.'

'Okay, fine. Then don't ask her to leave. But tell her to stop breathing down your neck all the time.'

'She doesn't breathe down my neck. That's just her way of showing she cares.'

'There is a difference between care and control. She keeps asking you to grow up but how come she never lets you?' Miss corporate bigshot disparaged. 'Why does she treat you like such a *moron*?'

This was too much – didn't Sangita understand boundaries? It was okay for me to crib about Amma but how dare she? Next she'd be asking me to become a man and grow a penis or something. Too late for that, I was already a mother.

'You're the one who treats me like a moron. Not Amma – and if she does treat me like a moron it's because you probably told her to. Just like you told her about sweet-dish Siddharth. How could you do that for god's sake?'

'Okay forget it, Suchitra. That was just a joke. I don't mean to upset you more. But your rebellion is futile – like a kid throwing tantrums.'

'How would you know about kids throwing tantrums?' As if she had one or was ever likely to have one. Miss Spinster forever Sangita.

'One doesn't have to be a mother to understand basic human psychology. I have to apply it in my workplace every day, you know. A bully recognizes the boy who cries wolf. And that, my dear, empowers them even more.'

Had Sangita been spying on my elaborate psychology notes? How on earth did she so easily know all the things I had spent the whole night researching before my parents arrived? *Oh I can show off too, girlfriend; watch me:*

'It's called Narcissistic Personality Disorder by the way, not the boy-who-cried-wolf syndrome. Get your facts right before showing off. And don't talk shit about my Amma. Don't you have any family values? How would you feel if I criticized your mom?

'Oh please. Stop being such a baby. And I suggest you tell your parents to give you a chance to grow up if that's what they so badly want for you.'

'It's not as if I'm not trying. It's just that like everything else in my life this one isn't working either.' I put on my best puppy dog expression again in the hope that it would shut Sangita up.

No such luck. Her voice grew more aggressive: 'Look, the next time Amma suggests you get a job ask her to do the same – one *other* than being your Amma.'

'Stop talking down to me the entire time, okay? I should have never let you in on my family secrets. Mind your own business.'

'I am not talking down to you. Try and understand what I am saying instead of taking off on some imagined insults. Just stop reacting and start acting. It's not that difficult.'

I felt pretty sure there was a name for the corporate success induced megalomania Sangita suffered from too. Or a term for a man trapped in a woman's body. I researched it as soon as she left.

'The megalomaniac differs from the narcissist in that he wishes

to be powerful rather than charming, and seeks to be feared rather than loved. To this type belong many lunatics and most of the great men of history.'

The quote was from Bertrand Russell.

I immediately called Sangita to share it with her.

'Listen, whatever, yaar – it's ultimately all up to us. And I'm tired of listening to your rubbish. God only helps those who help themselves.'

If it was up to me to help myself, of what use was god? I started to think once again of Shrink's ludicrous suggestion that Ganesha was a phallic symbol. *Chhee,* Chitty! Have some shame! How dare you think of *god* like that? The fact that you can see anything under his paunch shows how perverse and depraved you are. *Slap! Whack! Dishoom!*

Much as Sangita's words stung, I had to concede that what she said made sense. Definitely more than Shrink's hokum and my own intense research on the matter. Though I had rattled off all those words like 'Dementia Pugilistica' and 'Narcissistic Personality Disorder' I hadn't thought about them so much. It had only been to please and piss off Amma and Nana at the same time. It was time I started to think about how I *really* felt and what I wanted, rather than impressing myself and my oppressors with academia. *And I wanted marriage. And hugs! And …*

'See you soon. Thanks for your advice.'

I made my resolve then and there. I wasn't going to be the boy who cried wolf any more. I was going to be the girl who grabbed the bulls by its horns and grew into her own glory. I finally had a plan! *Action, no reaction, action, no reaction* I mumbled to myself, over and over again – like the Gayatri/ Shanti mantra I had grown up hearing.

I pulled out my diary and wrote down my itinerary for the following day.

This I called my 'U Go Girl' plan. UGG for short:

- Do pranayama deep breathing (action)
- Ignore Amma /Nana (no reaction)
- Take Kaveri to puppet class at 12 directly from math's tuition (action)
- Don't think. Don't think. Don't think so much (action+ no reaction? Not too suret…)
- Breathe in breathe out. Calm down (Action + action)
- Start dieting regardless of how much Amma cooks (action + no reaction)
- Don't forget past-life regression therapy session at 7.30 (action only)
- Remind Shrink of her 'buy three get one free' past-life therapy session offer. Insist. And don't pay up since you've already paid for the last few(action)
- Insist on free session in spite of sidetracking techniques bound to be employed (action + no reaction)

U Go Girl! UGG! Om shanti shanti hee!

The last line I obviously didn't number because…why didn't I number it? I couldn't exactly remember now. Should I have numbered it? Naah! U Go Girl was an attitude thing – not a to-do thing, or was it? And what if I forgot where I was supposed to go and ended up in the wrong place instead? Self sabotage not allowed; not in my UGG plan

♋

Amma watched me intently as I had my first cup of tea the following morning. Scrutinizing my trembling fingers and the way that they made the teacup rattle. She squinted hard, trying to get a better look at the nervous tics of my defiant head, obviously examining me for any further signs of inebriated dementia or Celine Dion drug side/after effects. She did this from vantage points across the house, as she chopped vegetables and cleaned the rice.

'That child is being deprived of nutritious food,' she sighed like the ultimate female martyr from one of her history books. I suggested she fry my brain instead of the potatoes she was peeling and then jump into the fire as it simmered. That way, she could be a true female martyr. A unique example of Sati. The first woman in Indian history who jumped into the funeral pyre of her daughter, instead of her husband's. Clap! Clap! Clap!

Amma didn't find it funny at all. Oink!

And so I had to acknowledge that point number two in today's itinerary i.e., Don't React to Amma /Nana *At All*, had failed at moment one. Even before I had had the time to execute point number 1 and do my pranayama breathing. Dang!

'Yaal ra kanna? Why are you behaving so strangely all the time? What is bothering you?'

I ignored her and completed task number 3, i.e. Drop Kaveri to Puppet Class.

Now time for point number 4.

Breathe in breathe out. Inhale exhale. Calm down. Calm down. *Relax!* Oh no – why was this part so difficult? But how could I possibly calm down when even my curtains and windowpanes were mocking and laughing at my inability to see any task through? I gave up. In sheer frustration I started bingeing on banana chips and Snicker bars. Thereby ensuring that point number 5 (i.e. Start Dieting) failed too.

Boo hoo! Self sabotage on UGG (U Go Girl) plan not allowed. Why wasn't anything working?

No *Shanti Shanti Shantee Shantee-hee tee-hee...*

'Relax, Suchitra – point number 5 has not failed entirely. Don't beat yourself up so much. Yes, you didn't start dieting as you had written down in today's UGG, but at least you didn't eat Amma's food either, right? So that means at least half of one of your eight points has succeeded right? 0.5 out of 8 is not bad really – it's a start,' Shrink said.

Really? Start to what? I had forgotten already. Dang! I would try and pick up those Ashwaganda memory pills from the chemist on the way back – if I remembered.

Shrink suggested that since the name UGG – U Go Girl! had a negative connotation (being an abbreviation for ugly and all) why didn't I consider changing it to GGU – for Go Girl U? 'You don't want to start feeling worthless again, do you? Now that would be self-sabotage, for sure. More than the fact that you couldn't complete all the tasks on your list.'

Gosh! GGU, was she mad? I needed to get with it and unleash my inner rockstar, not enrol in some Good Girl University

'So try GGU instead of UGG...*hmm*?' Shrink handed me the bill.

It was the quick gleam in her eyes as I dipped my hand into my purse to pay for the day's session that gave her away. Conniving bloody creature. Did she think I hadn't seen her casually drop her handkerchief over the last point in my schedule for today? Point number 9. Insist on Free Session In Spite of Sidetracking Techniques Bound to be Employed (action + no reaction).

GGU, my ass!

'Oh not 8 points, Shrink. Nine! You promised this session would be free, remember? And I'm very happy with my UGG plan – thank you very much.'

Action+ reaction+ no reaction = U Go Girl! Rocking! I was back on track again.

U Go Girl! UGG! Om shanti shanti hee!

♋

Amma prepared mountains of food every day, completely ignoring Kaveri's pleas that she didn't want to eat rasam rice *all* the time and could she please have some pasta instead?

'Amma, please don't cook. I have a very good cook to whom I pay a lot of money.'

I had even spent a substantial part of my hard-earned alimony and sent the cook to classes to train her in the art of fine western cuisine – gourmet pastas and burritos and flambé.

'What good cook? She doesn't know any cooking. Her sambar is unpalatable. Poor Kaveri, does she have to eat sambar made from readymade powder? Why employ a cook if they can't even make sambar and rasam powder at home? Is this any way to run a kitchen?'

My good cook of course threatened to leave every single day, sometimes even many times a day, tired of Amma's acerbic barbs. I tried my best to pacify Cook, make peace, and salvage the situation. After all, my life – like that of any other urban Indian woman's, especially a single mother's – was entirely dependent on my staff. Without them I became a housebound slave to my child and dogs and milkman and bread-man, who knocked on my door at regular half-hourly intervals.

Amma would be gone in a few days – as soon as she was satisfied that my alcohol-induced psychosis had abated. And when she was satisfied that I wasn't about to do anything stupid like marry a Muslim who looked like a goat, thereby jeopardizing her granddaughter's future forever.

How would I manage if my cook left? It had happened on one of Amma's prior visits – and I'd been left cooking, cleaning, walking the dogs, dropping and picking up Kaveri from the bus-stop, cooking and cleaning, walking the dogs again, answering doorbells, phone calls and then walking my dogs again, cooking, cleaning... *Uff!* My body started to tremble in memory of that. Inhale exhale, inhale exhale, Suchitra. Nothing bad is going to happen. Happiness is round the corner. Roll your tongue under your palate and breathe in breathe out, breathe in breathe out...

'Are your servants more important to you than your own mother?'

'Amma, please...' I was ready to bang my head against the wall in frustration.

'I am cooking for Kaveri. Not for you. That poor child is undernourished.'

Undernourished?! She was the tallest kid in class, almost a head above her classmates. And won gold medals in judo and basketball along with getting full A's in most subjects. My child was nutrition deprived?!

'That's because of the vitamin syrups you give her,' Amma threw them away. 'There is no need for them. She should get her strength naturally from her food.'

♋

Amma's vigil extended to other aspects of my life too. Like when Pankaj came over for one of our Scrabble sessions. 'Chittoo, that Gangotri fellow is here. Why has he come again?'

'What do you mean *why* has he come again? We plan to play Scrabble, that's why.'

'You can play Scrabble with your daddy also. Don't make excuses.'

'No I can't play with Nana. It's no challenge. I defeat him too easily.' It was my father who had started my Scrabble craze and my fascination with word games, which I played all through my childhood with cousins, uncles, aunts, Amma's scholar colleagues, and whoever entered our home. I never lost a game – until I played with Pankaj – that's why I felt like hugging him even more. A girl needs a man she can look up to, *na*?

'How can he defeat you at Scrabble? He is a cunning chap. He must have pretended to lose so that you get flattered and shed your inhibitions and give into his…'

'Stop it, Ma. Why can't I play if I want to?'

'Then you can play it with Shekhar also. Just because y'all are divorced doesn't mean he cannot play Scrabble with you. After all, you are the mother of his child. I will speak to him.'

'No, Shekhar refuses to play Scrabble because he doesn't like to lose. Especially to a woman. I'll tell you what – why don't you get Nana and Shekhar to play Scrabble, man to man, so I can get on with my Scrabble hugs woman to man?'

Amma obviously didn't hear the last part of my sentence. 'How can this Gangotri chap win if Shekhar also can't defeat you in Scrabble? I told you he's a cunning chap – all business people are. You better be careful.'

Not trusting me to do the needful and look after myself, Amma took charge the minute Pankaj was seated with me for a game. 'What is your qualification?' she demanded of him with alarming hostility.

'I'm a businessman,' Pankaj smiled. 'I have a jewellery business.'

'Yes, I know you're a businessman with a lot of money, Chittu told me that. That's why I'm asking you, what is your qualification? Till how much have you studied? Because money is not everything, you know.'

Pankaj smiled again, super amused. 'My family also runs a few schools and colleges, Mrs Krishnamoorthi. You should visit our faculty sometime – maybe even consider giving a few guest lectures...'

'Erm, Pankaj, Amma means, what's your *quartation*?' I was trying to murder Amma with my eyes but she wasn't looking at me. She continued to blaze at my Scrabbler.

'Amma is planning to buy some jewellery for me, you know – for my marriage,' I hammed furiously. 'So she wants to know what percentage of silver you mix in your gold. In our family we insist on purity – it's the most vital qualification for a bride to be...'

Now Amma shifted her wrathful eyes on to me.

'Oh, sorry, I forget to tell you' – I was enjoying this now; especially Amma's Yo Angry Mamma expression. How long would she continue to pummel me down? Couldn't she just leave me alone to Scrabble in peace? – 'Pankaj, you can stop looking for a husband for me now, *haan*,' I continued, with one eye on my glowering parent. 'Don't stress any more about that.'

'No, no stress at all,' Pankaj raised his hands, eyes pinging between me and Amma. WTF, exactly, was going on? Nana sat in the other room, solving the mid-day crossword.

'Yeah, I'm finally at peace now. You see, I've decided to

marry Muffin, my cocker spaniel. I proposed to him yesterday and he accepted,' I stroked Muffin under his chin and he licked me back playfully and rolled on his back, showing me his pink and white stomach to be tickled.

'See, Amma – I told you I'm a good girl who just wants to marry for company. And who better than a dog – man's best friend? Don't you agree Muffin is a better choice than Iqbal?'

Pankaj's eyes ping-ponged and rolled again...were Amma and me *fighting,* or was this supposed to be funny, or what? He was too polite to get up and sprint out of the door.

I elaborated that Muffin the cocker spaniel was a manglik – i.e. his Mars is placed in the 8th house of his horoscope – very bad aspect indeed for his spouse. Might just kill me on the wedding night, or something. So just to make sure nothing morbid like that happened and to negate the effects of Muffin's horoscope, I had decided to first marry him to the coconut tree in my building garden. 'So I'll need *two* sets of jewellery, *haan* Pankaj? One for Muffin's marriage to the tree; that can be simple – just a brooch or pendant that I'll stick into the tree. And the second should be more elaborate – earrings, necklace, mangalsutra the works. Because that's for me, *na*, and I've been waiting so long to be a bride...'

'Sure,' Pankaj laughed.

'And please make sure the gold is the best quality Pankaj. Everything in a bride *has* to be pure and untouched, right Amma?'

'*Chheh! Kharmon!*' Amma spat and muttered, 'I wish I had died before I saw my own daughter behaving like such a cheap mental case,' under her breath, in Telugu.

(The hierarchical history of mental cases in our family was

a top secret. Access to this information to outsiders was, is and will always be guarded fiercely. I wondered whether this was the right moment to tell Pankaj about Subu Mama the family genius too. Naah, that I would save for a more opportune time.)

But, then…OMG, I thought, what if the tree really died because I married 'Muffin the Manglik with the Exalted Mars?' And what if the environmentalists or Green Peace Society or SPCA got after me and put me behind bars before I had a chance to exchange my wedding vows?

No, couldn't risk that. Best I do it quietly and privately in the dead of night. I would wait for a week after Muffin married the coconut tree and then, whether or not the tree died, I would marry Muffin in an exclusive ceremony at home, attended by just my parents, the priest and Muffin's girlfriend, Cupcake.

Amma looked ready to slap me. I carried on in glee: 'I know what you're thinking, Amma. How am I even thinking of inviting Cupcake, the bitch, right? But why would I not? Did you think I would be jealous or something? Baah! How can I feel jealous of Cupcake, for god's sake? She's just a little bitch. I'm a grown woman now and know, with my newfound wisdom, that a dog will always run after a bitch in heat, don't I?'

'Chittu, if you don't stop this nonsense…'

'It's not nonsense, Ma. Listen, how is infidelity a dog's fault? It's the way god has made dogs. So I will always love Muffin anyway, whether he runs after Cupcake or another random bitch in heat on the street. So don't worry, this time around I'll definitely make my marriage work.'

I asked Amma to request Shekhar to give me away as the

bride in my marriage ceremony to Muffin since she shared such a good rapport with him and was so keen to set things right between us. I knew if I asked him directly he would pretend to be busy.

'If you consider her your friend why don't you try and drill some sense in Suchitra?' Amma turned to Pankaj pleadingly, all her previous aggression stunned into submission. Was I imagining it or did I glimpse the first dew of a tear in her eye? 'I cannot understand why she is behaving like this.'

'He is here to play Scrabble, Ma. Not to give me advice on my life. So can we get on with the game please?'

Amma's interference had made it impossible for me to think of a single decent word. I stared at the letter tiles on my rack. I deliberately played the word 'sex' for her to see.

'*Chheh*! *Vinaase kaale vipreet buddhi*', (a rotting mind leads to one's own downfall) Amma spat in sheer disgust. She stormed away noisily, appointing Nana – an able Watson to her Sherlock – to spy instead.

Nana proved to be a very alert sentinel following Amma's orders to the T. He stayed on even when Amma announced she was retiring to bed because she had a headache.

'Such, want to go out for dinner?'

I jumped at Pankaj's suggestion – now this seemed like a proper date, didn't it? No one had asked me out on a date in the longest time, or called me 'Such' in that caressing, lilting way before. It made my heart go all flippety-floppety. Forget the dinner, I intended to just grab him in a tight clinch the *minute* we stepped out the door. But Nana ensured that I couldn't. He followed me to the elevator and bored his eyes into mine. 'When are you getting back?'

'I don't know, Nana.'

The calls started even before we were seated at the restaurant.

'Are you drinking wine? How many glasses have you had already? Don't drink more than one, understood?'

'Nana, please, I am too old to be constantly told what to do. I am an independent woman leading my own life. Show some respect...'

'You are always going to be my baby, ra chilaka. I just want you to be careful that's all...'

'Why? Has Amma told you to tell me that or do you really care about me for a change?' I could feel the water well in my eyes.

Pankaj handed me a tissue to wipe my tears and suggested I switch off my phone so we could enjoy our dinner in peace. But how could I? What if Kaveri needed to get in touch with me? She did that often, afraid of the dark as she was. She needed to sleep with a night light on, even though Amma said it was unnecessary, insisting that she was old enough to sleep without it now.

Old enough, Amma? How about me?

The problem with bigots is they always justify their own warped ways by harping on the faults of others. Till the oppressed victim loses all her self-esteem and starts revering her very oppressors. That's why my siblings had never fought back. They had accepted their plight as their due. I wouldn't allow any of that rubbish to touch my daughter. I had told Amma to stop interfering in my life: 'A child who cannot feel safe in her own home will not have the emotional memory to feel safe anywhere,'– but to no avail.

I desperately needed a vacation to get away from it all.

'Why don't you come with me to Bangkok?' Pankaj suggested softly.

I wasn't sure I had heard him correctly! 'Are you crazy? You're a married man! Give me your phone. I'm going to call your wife right now and tell her about your shocking suggestion...'

'Chill,' he laughed. 'I'm going there on business for a day as it is. You could stay on. And you can have your own room... it's up to you.'

Of course, it was up to me. But how could I trust myself not to pounce on him and tear his clothes off the minute we stepped into the apartment? How would I continue to hide my inner demons successfully?

'Amrita is moving out next month...' Pankaj volunteered suddenly, sensing my discomfort, referring to his wife of many years. 'Our marriage is just not working out.'

Didn't all married men say that?

'What about your kids?' I knew that Pankaj's children were quite grown and away in hostels. Just like Chandni's daughter, who had been packed off to Aiglon in Switzerland at the age of seven. Can you imagine leaving a child on her own at such a tender age? But that's what the super-rich idle women often did; sent their kids away to boarding so they could shop and kitty in peace. On the advice of their super-rich husbands who couldn't spare the time for either – the wife or the kids.

'I hope Amrita knows how difficult it can be for a single woman living alone. What is she going to do?'

What she has always done,' Pankaj smiled. 'She'll shop some more, I guess.'

Oh, Amrita's shopping sprees were legendary; Chandni's Gucci bags niggardly compared to her lavish shopping extravaganzas. Known as the Shopping Czarina of Mumbai, Amrita had admitted in the front page of the *Bombay Times,* no less, that she had a shopping addiction. The word for it was 'Oniomania' – but how would the likes of her possibly know that? She wasn't a word-obsessed Southie like me; probably refused to play Scrabble with her husband too, because of her limited vocabulary. Which is why he had no choice but to seek me out.

I would explain that to my parents when I returned. What did they think? I was having sex with Pankaj in the restaurant under the table or what? *Chhee! Chitty! Did you just think about having sex with Pankaj? That too under the table?*

I quickly asked Pankaj a few more questions about his wife. All of a sudden it was awkward for me to even talk about her. The fact that I was having dinner with her husband, who had just asked me to go on a holiday with him, that too to Bangkok, (the global den of prostitution!), made me feel like a hooker already.

I decided even if I did ever go (which was of course not going to happen) I would pay for my own airfare and hotel room. That way even if we did end up having sex, he would be the slut and not I. But he would be a slut only if I footed his bill as well, *na*? *Can you afford that, Suchitra? Then what about your insomnia oil, Kaveri's scuba-diving holiday…haan?*

I twirled, blew on, and promptly toppled my bowl of chowder.

Sensing my panic, Pankaj immediately offered to drop me home. When Nana called for the fifth time asking once again when I would return and how many glasses of wine I had already consumed, I turned my phone off in sheer disgust. I would be home in a few minutes. I could do with some peace till then. Another moment of nagging and my head would detonate.

'I think my parents have understood me all wrong. When I said I don't want to be alone...I meant I needed...what I meant was... oh god! I really don't know what I think say or mean any more... How can I go to Bangkok with you? What sort of a girl do you think I am?'

'You could go there alone if you like. Let me know if you want me to make the arrangements. You don't have to stay at my apartment either, there are lovely spas in Bangkok, they will help you relax.'

His suggestion heightened my worry. Relax my foot – how could I? If I did yield to my shameful lusty temptation how would I explain where I was going to my family? *On an adulterous sex vacation with a married man?* No, no. it was impossible. Totally against my morally-sound, middle-class make up and fear of punishment by Amma, society and god himself.

The whole household was awake when I returned. 'Why did you put your phone off? Kaveri woke up and was asking for you,' my mother said.

I ignored Amma and Nana and took Kaveri to tuck her in to bed.

♋

The final straw was when Amma barged into my room two days later demanding, 'Why is that driver sitting on the sofa in the hall? I know you are modern and have lived in London for so many years and all that but this is India and this is too much.'

In Amma's book of desi staff etiquette, servants had to sit on the floor. I mean, how *dare* lackeys sit at a level of direct eye contact and not have to look up to her in fear and servitude?

The driver Amma was talking about was, of course, Sangita's newly-acquired boyfriend, M. Mascerenhas. A junior in her office. Someone she had pulled out of her cowboy hat only to prove that she wasn't a closet lesbian. I felt pretty sure of that. And to think that they – my girlies – had hidden the fact that Sangita was seeing Mohan from me for almost three months, because they didn't want me to feel any worse about my own manlessness.

It had got me scathing mad with them. 'Feel bad? Are you crazy? I would rather die a born-again virgin! Does your mother know? Is *that* why she had a stroke and was hospitalized for the last few weeks?' I called up Sangita's mother to commiserate. Moments later, Sangita was on the phone to me.

'Are you crazy, Suchitra? How can you tell my mother something like you always thought I was a lesbian? Sangita was aghast. 'You've really lost it.'

'Well, how could you tell my Amma that I asked total stranger sweet-dish Siddharth to leave his *chaddi choomchee* wife and marry me?' I rejoindered, nonchalantly.

That's what had convinced Amma that I had jumped off the rails and plunged headlong into the devils' waiting arms and made her tighten the reins of her smothering vigil.

'That was a *joke...*'

Oh really, girlfriend? Ha ha. Sooo damn funny!

'And my mother doesn't interfere in my personal life. She respects the fact that I'm a grown up, capable of making my own decisions. Unlike yours...' Sangita sneered.

Apparently, her mother had smiled benignly on being introduced to Sangita's newly-acquired boyfriend. Unlike Amma, who had glared so hard at Pankaj the other night, when he'd dropped me home after dinner, that he had beat a hasty retreat fearing an honour killing, or something.

'*Aiyyo* – boyfriend, aa? He looks young enough to be her son. And is Sangita not a Bengali Brahmin? This fellow looks like a schedule-caste. Why can't you find yourself some better friends?' Amma was at her disapproving best.

'Amma, please, how can you talk about caste in today's date and age? If somebody heard you, you'd be arrested. You should be happy that she has found someone...' Even though I didn't feel happy about it at all, I managed to squeeze an 'I'm-so-happy-for-Sangita' gleam in my downcast-with-sorrow eyes.

It seemed to me that things were working out for everybody except me.

How come?

When would *I* find my true love?

Where? Why? Or why not?

God, are you listening?

What am I supposed to do now?

9

It was called 'Om Harmonics', or some such blah – a new breakthrough in meditation techniques, Sangita had said – and I really shouldn't have gone, but at the time it had seemed my only escape from the tension I had begun to feel when Pankaj had suggested we go to Bangkok to relax.

I needed it bad; to relax, that is.

'It will turn your monkey brain into a Buddha. It's worked for me, baby,' Sangita had grinned, entwining her hand in Mohan's as he drove us to our meditation class.

I looked at her in disgust. Didn't this woman have any shame? Wasn't the fact that she had got herself a boyfriend who looked like her son – actually make that her driver's son – bad enough? Did she have to grin so lasciviously? The glances they exchanged, as I watched from the backseat, were making my stomach churn. I was about to barf. Boyfriend, my foot. Corporate casting couch was more like it.

My finely honed, middle-class, moral make up was further piqued when we screeched to a halt at the gas station. Sangita fished out the cash, no questions asked. Mohan grinned. Gave her a kiss on the nose! Yuck, gross! Didn't he notice her nostril hair? Now I knew how she had managed to get herself a boyfriend, while I was still struggling solo. She was *paying* for it, that's how. Bloody cougar!

Still, going for the class was a better option than Amma's

incessant nagging. I had no other place to run. Besides, it was cheaper than Shrink's fee.

♋

In the meditation class, I struggled to keep my eyes closed and focus on the task at hand, i.e. harnessing my monkey brain and transcending to the divine plane.

The meditation guru, who looked like Dracula in drag – actually make that Cher in a bad guru impersonation – patted me on the top of my head kindly. She urged me to close my eyes as everyone else was doing. I wondered how they could all sit so still. And I wondered how it had never dawned on me before that Cher actually did look like Dracula in female costume – all that was missing were the vampire fangs. The revelation of the resemblance made me gasp.

'Do you believe in life after love?' I asked the Lady Dracula/ Cher-as-guru-impersonator.

'Huh?'

I decided to go easy on the questions and tried to sit still. The not moving was driving me insane. Never had I felt a stronger urge to scratch the middle of my back. I fished out a comb from my purse and tried to reach the centre of my spine to quell the itch.

Lady Dracula took the comb out of my hand and put it away along with my purse, at the far end of the room.

'Calm down,' she cooed, 'and close your eyes.'

I looked at her more intently.

The mangalsutra – pious sign of one's marital status – around Lady Dracula/Cher-in-drag's neck brushed against my cheek – the cold metal eliciting a sharp sting. Great! I felt sure

Sangita had invited me here just to prove how pathetic I was. Even Draculas and dykes could get themselves husbands and boyfriends while I couldn't even pull off a date – as my last outing with Pankaj had clearly shown.

When Nana had called me for the seventh time, I had just burst into tears and asked Pankaj to take me home. Now I fought the urge to snatch the mangalsutra off her neck and steal it for my own marriage ceremony. That would make Amma even happier – marrying a dog with stolen jewellery.

'Calm down...' Lady Dracula/Cher-in-drag whispered again.

Calm down? How on earth *could* I? She would appear in my nightmare tonight for sure, sucking my sad, single, blood. I tried to resume the scratching of the centre of my back with my fingertips as soon as she had turned her face away. The itch was rabid. Dang! Why was the spot so hard to reach? I tried *chuch-chuchuing* the zoned-out zealot behind me to scratch my back but she didn't cut me any slack.

I noticed it first as a tingling that started in the outer ear – like a cellphone on vibrate. It crept into my skull, meandering through the cortex, layer by layer, one into the other, overlapping, under-sliding, up and down and round and around, emerging back into my throat, filling my mouth and taking possession of my jaw.

I felt like a cat was nudging and purring against me. Soon the itch in my lower back was forgotten completely as my trembling jaw line took precedence, and then – *zap! zap! pause zoom! zap! zap!* – the frequency of the tremors started to increase at an alarming pace.

I glanced at the faces around me, zombied out in Zen, beatific smile on their faces. It made me giggle.

Shush, Suchitra. Was this the effect of the meditation?

If it was truly the power of Om, this was one helluva trip – would tell Amma about it for sure. I didn't need any rave parties in Goa to go into a psychedelic jerk fest. Om Harmonics was a far superior drug than the Celine Dion variety. I would insist Amma try it soon

Zap! zap! tingle! tingle! pause zap! zap! zoom! The room slanted into a diagonal angle. I felt myself losing balance and keeling over. Why wasn't anybody else in the room falling down? The tremors moved into my thorax and my gut, filling my body with prick-points of undeniably, pointy, prickly sensations. *Zap! zap! zoom! zoom! zoom! zap! zap!...* OMG – this was getting a bit much. I started to cackle:

Mmmmmpphh...

OOOOOOOOO

MMMMMMMM

♋

Soon the rattle in my jaw spread further down, past my collar bones, through my thorax, into my pelvis, descending into my thighs, legs, feet, toes. Then suddenly, changing direction, it yanked itself back, ascending in the same direction it had descended and exploded into my skull. My body started to convulse vigorously as if plugged into a live electric socket. *Zap! zap! pause zap! zap! zoom!* Shake, rattle and roll. Shake, rattle and roll! Shssshhhhh........

OOOOOOOOOOO

MMMMMMMMM

GGGGGGGGG!!

I started to laugh uncontrollably.

My body crumpled, in an acute stomach spasm.

'Suchitra, are you okay?' Lady Dracula looked alarmed, her arms extended out towards me like vicious talons.

Of course I'm not okay. Do I look okay to you? I knew exactly what I had. What did she think I was? A dum dum? I had researched this too along with Dementia Pugilistica and other psycho stuff the minute I knew my parents were descending on me.

I know the list by heart too, Lady Dracula. Never underestimate the knowledge thirst of a terrified soul:

Atychiphobia	–	fear of failure.
Anuptaphobia	–	fear of being single.
Cacophobia	–	the fear of ugliness.
Athazagoraphobia	–	fear of being forgotten or ignored.
Erotophobia	–	fear of sexual love.
Hamartophobia	–	fear of sinning.
Isolophobia	–	fear of solitude, being alone.
Lysssophobia	–	fear of rabies or of becoming mad.
Mnemophobia	–	fear of memories.
Murophobia	–	fear of mice.
Rhytiphobia	–	fear of getting wrinkles.
Panophobia	–	fear of everything
Paraskavedekatriaphobia	–	fear of Friday the 13th.
Sociophobia	–	fear of society or people in general.
Syngenesophobia	–	fear of relatives.
Odontophobia	–	fear of teeth or dental surgery.
Obesophobia	–	fear of gaining weight.
Pogonophobia	–	fear of beards.

Polyphobia	– fear of many things.
Nostophobia	– fear of returning home.
Peccatophobia (Imaginary crime)	– fear of sinning.

Ha ha ha. Tee hee hee. I couldn't stop laughing in spite of the cramp in my abdomen – I doubled up and guffawed into the floor.

'Calm down,' Lady Dracula breathed down on me, her mangalsutra brushing my cheek again. This time I tried yanking it off her neck. She struggled back, clinging onto it with all her might. It made me laugh louder. I grabbed her robe and wiped my nose and mouth on it.

Calm down?

To what end?

How would that make me happy?

I had been calm and happy all those years so many years ago when I was an ignorant, innocent, blissed-out London housewife, baking cookies and waiting for my husband to return home – hot food on the table and all – how did it help me in any way?

Lady Dracula looked horrorstruck, her mouth agape. I laughed some more, unable to take my eyes off her vulva-shaped pout. I reached out to touch it – she squinched, petrified.

I carried on laughing. I knew exactly what I would tell Amma when I got back home – this meditation class had been a good idea after all; it jogged my memory and provided me with answers to questions long buried.

'Do you know the meaning of the word "cunnilingus"?' I let go of Lady Dracula's mangalsutra and patted her robe down in apology. Her brow creased apropos to her displeasure.

'How can you teach meditation and look so pissed off at the same time, Lady Dracula? Don't you see the paradox in that?' I guffawed, continuing to stare at the red gash of her lips. 'So tell, *na*, do you know the meaning of the word "cunnilingus"?'

She ordered me to leave the room at once. I was disturbing the other people's concentration. What? I was being punished again?

'*Why?* N*ooo*... you can't do that, Madame Meditation,' I said in a French accent which made me giggle even more. 'Please let me be happy,' I tittered. 'But that would be your failure, wouldn't it? If I got happy, why would I need to come to your meditation class along with all the other sad people here? I would be blissfully free and dancing on the rooftop in the rain and ...'

'I think you need to step out, darling...'

'You know, I'm such a bad girl that Amma didn't talk to me for a month when I said the word "cunnilingus"?'

Lady Dracula looked mortified as she tried to scrape my shaking-with-laughs body off the floor. I resisted.

'How was I to know the meaning then? I was only thirteen...' I didn't *care* if the whole class was being disturbed. This meditation was an oxymoron too. Why did you have to struggle so hard to concentrate to relax so that you could then concentrate on other things that robbed you of your peace?

'...and a half. *Such* a baby.'

'You poor thing,' Lady Dracula hoicked me by the arm and led me outside. 'You must have been very upset. I can see that's what's troubling you – why didn't she talk to you?'

She turned back to the class and instructed them to carry on omming, lifting her palms up like an opera conductor as she led me out:

OMMMMM

OMMMMM...the class repeated after her, and closed their eyes again, happy to see me exit.

'No, no, I wasn't upset that Amma didn't talk to me for a month,' I collapsed, rolling on the floor, laughing outside the class. The itch was returning, I asked Lady Dracula to run her talons down the middle of my back. She obliged. Aaah that felt better. I leaned my back against the wall and explained my predicament through hiccupping hee haws: 'You see, I was not upset that Amma didn't talk to me for a month. I was upset that I wasn't as *lucky* as my brother Sudhakar, whom Amma didn't talk to for a year.'

Tears of laughter rolled down my cheeks. I clutched my stomach remembering that day vividly.

♋

My parents had returned from a hard day's work. As Amma busied herself with organizing the evening meal, Nana lounged on the drawing room settee solving the crossword puzzle in the mid-day newspaper. Sunita was busy learning Indian classical music with her Guruji inside. Elder sis Sujata was married and gone to Muscat – far, far away. Sudhakar lived in the medical college hostel. We seldom saw much of him any more, wrapped up as he was in surgical emergencies and serious scholarly stuff like that. It was just me and Nana as usual. Playing our, 'What's-the-new-word-today' game. I was thirteen and a half.

'*Chickuh chickuh chickuh chikah – Getti vaadu nenu, getti vaadu nenu*'

'*Chickuh chickuh chickuh chickuh chickuh – What a clever man I am, such a clever man I am...*' Nana sang tunelessly every time he got a piece of the crossword puzzle right.

Nana was such an awful singer one had to concentrate hard on the lyrics to figure out what song he was singing. This one, the *Getti Vaadu Nenu,* was easy. Only because it was his own composition and he sang it every single day. But any other song was impossible. Especially when he couldn't remember the lyrics and hummed a *la la la* instead and asked us to guess the song. That was pure torture.

'*La la la lalalala nananana lalala*...which song am I singing?'

'Please, Nana – how can I guess? All your tunes sound the same.'

'*La la la la la la la la. Mera mehboob aaya hai...*' It was the only Hindi song Nana knew.

'Oh you mean, "*Baharon phool barsao – mera mehboob aaya hai?*"'

'Correct, correct.' Nana would laugh. 'Poor fellow, couldn't he find someone better than an *aayah* to fall in love with?' Nana always found his own jokes funnier than anybody else ever did.

'*Chickuh chickuh chickuh chikah – getti vaadu nenu, getti vaadu nenu.* What word have you learnt today, ra kanna?' Nana stroked my hair as I sat by his side, lapping up all the love. These evening times were my most favourite of all. When I actually felt like I was part of a normal family. Our little haven, where the *chaddi choomchees* and Shambu Chinayna's of the world had no place. Amma's nightingale voice singing a Lata Mangeshkar song in her high-pitched soprano in sharp contrast to Nana's tuneless bray was pure manna from the skies. The effect was awesome – psychedelic almost. It was the only time, when she sang that is, that Amma seemed like an angel. Yes this was heaven for sure, and I the little cherub.

'What, no word today? What have you been up to?' Nana asked again.

Every day I learnt a new word or two from the new dictionary and thesaurus I had been gifted on my thirteenth birthday. My heart swelled with pride when Nana thumped me on the back each time I rattled off big words like 'percolate', 'askance' and 'skewed'. 'Try some bigger words next time,' Nana suggested.

That's exactly what I had intended to show off today. Since Tanaya (yes, the same one who looked like Elizabeth Taylor) had borrowed my dictionary for the day to complete her English essay. I had asked Deepak, one of the building boys for a word earlier that evening. Now he was already twenty-something and Amma and Nana didn't like me mixing with the older boys in the building, but I had never understood why. We always hung around in a group of all ages – boys and girls. How could I possible tell one of them, 'Sorry, you're not my age and I can't talk to you because Amma says all boys are bad?' Besides, Deepak was my badminton partner. We had even won the inter-colony mixed doubles tournament a few months ago. Even though Under 18 was a different category he had got me to enrol in the older category insisting I had the build and strength for it. That much was true. I had achieved full height and maturity at the age of ten – a fact that made some of my classmates in my 'girls only' school tease me for being a 'giant' and 'overgrown'. Deepak said it was probably because they were jealous that I was so pretty and even gave me ice-cream treats every time we won a match. How did any of this qualify as bad, just because he was a boy? How was that his fault? Though I had to admit the way he stared at me sometimes did make me feel a bit weird and flushed.

I showed Nana the word Deepak had scribbled down on a piece of paper happily. It was an eleven-letter word – my biggest ever. Even though I didn't know the meaning, I would find out as soon as Tanaya returned my dictionary. She hadn't done so before my parents arrived from work as promised but that was okay. Traffic in Mumbai was a nightmare even in the eighties.

I waited eagerly for Nana's thump of praise. But one look at his face and I knew something was terribly wrong. Nana's face had turned white.

'Where did you get this word from?' Nana seldom raised his voice but when he did it spelt doom.

My heartbeat accelerated.

Since I had already been warned not to spend my playtime downstairs in the building with the likes of Deepak, or any other boy for that matter, I held my tongue. It would mean I would be grounded and I didn't want that. 'Where did you learn this word?' Nana asked again.

I sensed something worse when Nana refused to even tell Amma the meaning of the word. Why was Nana looking so embarrassed? Or was he angry? His expressions, like his tunes, were hard to decipher.

Amma blazed fire at me. What had this disobedient, impertinent, precocious Chitty done now? Tanaya rang the doorbell at that very moment, dictionary in hand. Amma snatched the dictionary from her, banging the door shut on her face and flipped the pages to words starting with 'Cun'.

'Cunnilingus?! Who taught you this word?'

My heart was in my mouth: 'What does it mean?

Slap! Whack! Dishoom!

'What have I done wrong?'

'Shut up! Just shut up and answer my question. Who gave you this word?' *Slap Whack! Dishoom!* again. 'I told you, Nana, that Chittu is going out of control and I don't like her sitting with all those older boys downstairs. Her character is getting ruined...'

'I don't hang around only with the older boys. They are all part of the group. And they are not aliens...'

'Don't try and pretend to be so innocent. What have you been up to? And why are you wearing lip gloss?'

'I'm not wearing lip gloss. It's lip balm. I have to use it after my lips got so badly chapped on our Kashmir holiday. (A fact that Amma hadn't bothered to notice or rectify.) Sujata had sent the balm to me when I'd complained that my lips burned so much I could barely open my mouth. Just as she had got me to wear suitable inners when I'd confessed to her that badminton practice was getting uncomfortable – especially the way Deepak sometimes stared.

'Stop back-answering me. Nana, are you just going to sit there and let her talk to her mother so rudely?'

'I will not stop back-answering if you don't tell me what I have done wrong! Just because you don't know any big words and you are jealous that Nana spends all his time in the evenings with me and not with you.'

'Shut up. *Gunjullu!* Now! ' Amma barked.

I stood there still as a rock. I wasn't going to obey orders without understanding what I was being punished for again. *Slap! Whack! Dishoom!* some more. *Ouch!*

'A hundred...' Amma shouted. 'And not straight *Gunjullu*, understood? You have to alternate it with cross *Gunjullu*.'

'*Gunjullu*' is sit-ups or squats. In Hindi it is known popularly as 'uthak-baithak'. Which, when it became a form of punishment (like when you did the sit-ups holding your ears in repentance or just squatted on your haunches endlessly till your thighs caved in and knees collapsed) was 'murga' or chicken.

Now, those familiar with the punishment – i.e. murga or chicken, which is what *Gunjullu* originally was – will no doubt wonder what the big deal is in having to do some squats. It's good for muscle tone too. Every Indian kid has been through this punishment, in one version or the other, at some stage of their childhood – in fact, local schools are notorious for it.

But like everything else connected with Amma, her *Gunjullu* came with a twist. Double twist, alternately applied. In Amma's brand of *Gunjullu* we were not supposed to just hold our ears – that was kid stuff – a minor punishment. Definitely not cruel enough to punish heinous crimes like using vulgar words such as 'cunnilingus' and talking to older boys in spite of being warned not to.

In Amma's *Gunjullu* we were supposed to squat, holding our ears, and then slap our cheeks every time our hips almost touched the floor. And in one variation of cross *Gunjullu* we had to cross our hands and slap our cheeks with every alternate squat.

It went something like this: *Hold your ears and squat – slap your cheeks with our own hands – say sorry – rise. Hold your ears and squat – cross your wrists and slap your cheeks with your own hands – say sorry – rise.*

'Why are you saying sorry so softly? I can't hear you!' Amma thundered.

Pull your ears hard – squat – cross your wrists and slap your cheeks – say sorry – rise.

'The sorry is loud enough now, but why have your slaps gone so feeble? Let me hear the crack of your fingers against your cheek. Louder you shameless, unrepentant, characterless creature! *Louder*!'

It was not until I dug out the scrap of paper on which Deepak had written the word from the trashcan later that night that I learnt the meaning of the word 'cunnilingus'. I read it over and over, trying to drown out the angry screaming voices of my parents fighting in their bedroom inside. Amma shouted that it was all Nana's fault that I had become wayward. I couldn't hear Nana's voice over my own tears and thudding heart.

Cunnilingus is an oral sex act performed on a female. It involves the use by a sex partner of the mouth, lips and tongue to stimulate the female's clitoris, vulva, or vagina. A female may receive cunnilingus as part of foreplay before sexual intercourse, during intercourse, or as intercourse. The term is derived from the Latin words for the vulva (cunnus) and tongue (lingua).

OMG! No wonder Amma had been so angry! And poor Nana – his embarrassment was totally understandable. Oh no! What had I done? I should have obeyed Amma and stuck to my gang of girlfriends; she had been right about boys. I would never talk to that stupid Deepak again and tell him to go to hell and find himself another doubles partner.

Sunita held ice-cubes wrapped in a napkin against my cheek as I cried into her shoulders. As expected I was grounded. No going down to play and no what's-the-new-word with Nana any more, either.

Neelawwa explained that it was a very common form of

punishment in the villages down south. It's how they were all raised. Even erring adults had to perform this act of repentance in the presence of righteous adults. Amma was punishing me in the same way she herself had been punished – it was nothing personal.

Nothing personal?! My face, my cheeks, all puffed up and bruised, but I was not supposed to take it personally? However, keeping family secrets was vital, so maybe Neelawwa was right.

I told teacher that I had walked into a wall when I tried to help myself to some ice-cream in the middle of the night without remembering to turn the lights on. And that's why my face was swollen. 'You know, Miss Munshi, my Nana got me a one litre jar of my favourite ice-cream – Chocó walnut – I couldn't resist. This is what happens, *na,* when we get greedy?' Tanaya averted her eyes.

I had heard Sujata use such excuses often – the Morse code of the ashamed and petrified:

'*Tap! tap! slap! slap!* – I banged my head against the wall...'

'*Tap! tap! whack! whack!* – My cat scratched me and my doll...'

'*Tap! tap! dishoom! dishoom!* – I fell down the stairs...'

Teacher bought my excuse easily – she had obviously no knowledge of this brand of Morse code, or how to deal with children who had constant headaches and cried on their desks every other day.

When Sujata came down on her next holiday from Muscat she promptly confronted the building rogue. 'Stay away from my baby sister you pervert,' she said slapping Deepak tightly across the face. My big sister had a great way of dealing with stupid boys – being a stunning beauty and never rebelling against Amma's commands, she had learnt to keep them at bay in her own unique way. She vented all her aggression outside the house. Her slaps were famous in the entire neighbourhood. Deepak stayed away from me forever after that.

My big brother Sudhakar chose Andrology as his super specialty not too long after this incident, travelling the world extensively to study a subject as yet unrecognized in India. Andrology is to sexual male health what gynaecology is to a woman's, dealing with matters like erectile dysfunction and ways to enhance sexual health. He went on to become one of the world's experts on the subject. With a surgical technique recognized by the international medical fraternity and known all over the world as the Krishnamurti technique – to cure Peyronie's disease.

'What is this Peyronie's disease?' My parents had asked him just that one time when he'd won the prestigious Herbert Newman international award, and made the headlines. 'And when and why did you change the spelling of your surname?'

'The Peyronie's disease procedure is a dermal-flap operation to cure impotence...'

'*Impotence*, aa? *Chheh! Kharmon!* Of all the branches of medicine and surgery ...what is the need for all this? '

Sudhakar never explained his choice – and my parents were too embarrassed to raise the point ever again. Maybe it was to teach the Ammas of the world that there was no shame in the human body or in the natural sexual urge. And to educate the Nanas of the world, that, for a family to survive, it was vital to take a stand; to protect the vulnerable who depended on their power. This theory is of course my random conjecture. I have never asked Sudhakar about it either.

Random conjecture...*hmm* interesting use of words, Suchitra, you psycho chick...I started playing with my cigarette-lighter, moving it tantalizingly close to Lady Dracula's face, and imagined setting the place ablaze.

'I think you should take your friend home,' Lady Dracula told Sangita as soon as she emerged out of the Om Harmonics meditation class, looking like a blissed-out Buddha.

'What happened, Suchitra?'

'I drank too much water today.' My shirt was drenched in tears even though I was laughing away to kingdom come. 'It's made my brain so cloudy, it's raining through my eyes...'

Sangita dragged me to the car. She and Mohan went at each other again. *Muah! Muah! Puchak! Puchak!* I squeezed my eyes shut, placed my fingers over my ears, and clamped my lips together just like Gandhiji's three Hear-no-evil, See-no-evil, Speak-no-evil monkeys. But when Mohan whispered, 'Your looking so hot after this yoga class, ya baby,' so loud that my eardrums almost cracked, I couldn't bear it any more. What was Mohan – one of the three blind mice from the nursery rhyme? 'Stop, stop the car, Sangita! I need to buy something...'

'We are almost home. I don't think you're in any state to...'

'No, stop the car right now and let me get off.'

'Why? What do you want? I'll get it for you.'

'I need to buy a lollipop for your baby boy.'

Which is why I didn't object when Amma asked her, 'Sangita, what is the age difference between you and this Mohan fellow?'

'Erm... why Aunty?'

'He looks very young, that's why.'

'Well, he is. He's thirteen years younger than me. And since I'm pretty young myself that makes him very, *very* young.'

'*Aiyyo* – thirteen, aa? Don't you think that's too much? One or two I can understand, even up to five is still okay. But *thirteen* – my god! Doesn't your mother have any objection?'

'Thanks for your concern, Aunty, but my mother is fine about it.'

'Are you sure? Are you planning to marry this chap? Does she know that Mascerenhas means he's a schedule-caste convert? Y'all are Brahmins, no?'

Oh crap. Now Amma was pushing it. 'Amma, why do you always interfere so much? You better learn to talk to my friends properly.' I said it like I was angry, though deep down I was happy. Maybe it would teach Sangita a lesson or two on maintaining boundaries and not killing me with her PDA. She was doing that just to make me jealous, I was sure, while all the time pretending to care so much.

'*Aiyyo*, Sangita, I don't know what has happened to Chittu. Why don't you try and talk some sense into her? She gets angry with me for everything. What is wrong in what I asked you just now?'

'Nothing, Aunty.'

'What nothing? How can you go on about schedule-caste and Brahmin and all that crap? You're always talking shit and then feigning innocence. Like what you said about Pankaj, too,' I pointed out.

'I am your mother. It is my duty to tell you the truth. That fellow is cunning and I don't like him...'

'No, Ma – wrong again. Pankaj is not cunning. He's cunni*lingus*...'

Ha ha ha.

10

Amma always said that all she had ever prayed for, through each of her pregnancies, was that that her children didn't inherit her sister-in-law's (Nana's sister) *ondrakannu* (squint) and Nana's own *apaswaram* (off-key) vocal cords.

Amma's prayers had been answered.

All four of us were born with clear, large eyes and sang pretty well too. My middle sister, Sunita, went on to do an MA in Hindustani classical music and is now a teacher in that subject, much to her parents' delight – even though they would have *preferred* her to be a Carnatic music proponent rather than choose the Hindustani classical stream, which is a north Indian rather than South Indian genre. Sunita was the other musical genius in the family after Madurai Mani Mama – whose Carnatic music *kacheris*/concerts were attended by us every time we went to Chennai.

As for me, singing Hindi pop songs…

Pop!? How can you even *call* that music?

According to Amma, and all the other myopic, self-professed music experts in the family, classical music was the only credible genre worth performing or enjoying. Pop music was sheer noise; just another excuse to put young girls in skimpy clothes.

And though I wrote my own songs and sang them pretty darn good, I had to concede that my Pop's (Nana's) brand of music was sheer cacophony. (Sometimes I wonder if I married Shekhar because his singing was as atrocious as Nana's. They say, *na,* we tend to choose spouses that remind us of our parents? Because the human mind chooses situations and people it is most familiar with when young.)

But I wasn't that young any more.

So how come this thick smog of disorientation still refused to clear up?

♋

That's why Shrink had insisted I do a few past-life regression sessions; when the regular ones to calm me were providing no breakthroughs at all in my 'Heal-me-from-this-crazy-confusion' chaos.

Now, just for your information, past-life regression sessions are three times the price of the regular ones. I had not understood Shrink's greedy intentions then as I do now. If I had I would have flatly refused.

Because it was only on the sixth or seventh attempt at deep, deep hypnosis/past-life therapy sessions (having fallen fast asleep in all the ones prior) that I had any past-lifetime sightings at all. In which my conscious brain melted into my subconscious brain and subsequently regressed into my cosmic brain.

From brain, to womb, to foetus, to soul. Back to the sky and then in reverse, from soul, to womb, and foetus to brain.

In the last breakthrough session, which we will now call my 'Eureka session' for easy recall, Shrink had to actually pour half a bucket of water on me to bring me back from the dead into my present life. I couldn't believe what I had seen.

That was me? *Impossible!* How could I have been an evil king in my past life who went around killing little children for no reason at all? No way, Shrink, this was bull. But Shrink suggested rather firmly that maybe this previous life's 'Cruel-king-killing-little-children' aspect of my cosmic conscious brain had messed up my present life's subconscious and conscious brain.

But how could I blindly buy Shrink's theory that it could be those poor kids I had killed in my last life, who had now come back as Amma and Nana and Shekhar, et al, to take revenge and kill me before my brain had a chance to progress into adulthood? Just as I had done to all of them in our past lifetime together?

If that were the case why did god let me grow so old before he revealed this shocking past-life karma to me? Couldn't he have let Amma kill me with her anger at age thirteen-and-a-half itself?

Naah! Baah! Shrink was talking crap. I would figure this out for myself.

It took me three full days and six anxiety candles to come up with a theory of my own. After much breathe in breathe out, inhale exhale, twisting the tongue into a U and all I had my answer:

'Shrink...I'm thinking...maybe the evil king that I was – or rather that the world saw as evil – was actually a clairvoyant/mystic/psychic/tarot-reader type guy, who could see the future? And since he saw a bleak, marriage-less future for these kids he decided it was best to kill them off in childhood to save them the pain of loneliness in adulthood? So, *actually*, I was doing those kids I killed in my past life a favour?'

'Erm, what *exactly* do you mean, Suchitra? I'm not sure I understand what you're saying,' Shrink tilted her head to the side, scratched her pencil against her nose, and stared at me intimidatingly.

'Shrink, it's easy. What I'm trying to say is, when you're a kid and unhappy and all, you can always live on in the hope that one day you'll grow up and get out of this misery and everything will be well, can't you? After all, we are fed on fairy-tales and stories of knights in shining armour coming and sweeping us off our feet and whisking us into the sky. The happily-ever-after syndrome.'

'Are you sure these fairy-tales existed in the era when you were the evil king?'

Dang! Was my past-life evil king avatar BC or AD? The Brothers Grimm, creators of the 'happily-ever-after', were definitely AD – eighteenth century or something. However, the evil-king, Mahabharata outfit, with crown and all, that I had seen myself in, in my regression session, looked positively BC. *Hmm*...I hadn't thought about that. But Shrink was supposed to let me talk, that's what I was paying her for, wasn't I? So she would bloody well listen. I blustered on: 'Let me finish saying what I have to say, Shrink, please. It's important.

What was I saying? '*Haan,* about growing up on fairy-tales and happily-ever-after stories, and all. So, like, when you're a child, there's always hope. But when you're grown-up and still in the same befuddled place and you know that there's no one coming to rescue you, and there's not that much time left for your happily-ever-after life, what do you do? When all you have is yourself? And so you wonder if it's an easier option to just curl up and die...'

My argument was losing steam. Shrink's scepticism of my plausible theory sending my brain cells into disarray again. My voice grew feeble. Shrink pursed her lips and let me blabber on for a bit more:

'Because, by then you're bruised and battered self has forgotten that you are capable of anything but sorrow – it becomes an addiction. Curable only by marriage.' I didn't notice the tears streaming down my cheeks. Shrink handed me a tissue. I blew my nose

'Why are you talking about things like curling up and dying again, Suchitra? That's the problem with you artist types – you glamorize death like it's some sort of game. It's not a game you can afford to play – not with Kaveri around.'

OMG! Shrink was right! Is that why god had made me a mother with nothing else to do in this life? So I could finally fathom exactly how cruel it was to kill little children in my last life?

But then Shrink said we would discuss this past-life thingee in a later session since my brain was tired and incapable of making another journey there today. She said I needed to calm down first.

But when I got back from Lady Dracula's Om Harmonics class I'd realized, I didn't need to calm down.

I needed to get angry.

Real angry.

Mean angry.

Rock-star, *bad-ass* angry.

So I could muster up the courage to avenge myself against all those who irritated the life out of me, and sent my brain into a rattling tailspin!

This putting my girlies and Amma, and Shrink and Ramu *et al* in the room and setting it ablaze was a good plan – though not foolproof. How could I achieve that? i.e. make it error free?

So I didn't get caught and sent to jail and Kaveri wouldn't be left alone to fend for herself?

I racked my brain and scratched my jaw and stared hard at the computer screen trying to research my 'wannabe-a-vengeful-bad-ass' plan. My eyes were getting blurry but yet I pérsisted late into the night, ensuring the door was locked to avoid interruptions.

It was the blinking light of the sms from Sangita on my phone that sparked off the idea.

'Hey, drama queen, feeling any better?'

I typed in 'queen' and did a Google search. So what if my god had abandoned me, there was still Google. Aha! I quickly found both the queens I was looking for:

THE BANDIT QUEEN – PHOOLAN DEVI

In 1979, a gang of dacoits abducted Phoolan. The gang-leader, Baboo Gujjar, who was an upper-caste Gujjar, wanted to rape her. However, she was protected by Vikram, the deputy leader of the gang who belonged to Phoolan's caste, Mallah. One night when Baboo attempted to rape Phoolan, Vikram killed him and assumed the gang leadership. Phoolan became Vikram's second wife. The gang ransacked the village where Phoolan's husband lived. Phoolan stabbed her estranged husband, and dragged him in front of the villagers. The gang left him lying almost dead by the road, with a note as a warning for older men who marry young girls.

THE VIRGIN QUEEN – ELIZABETH OF ENGLAND

Elizabeth's unmarried status inspired a cult of virginity. In poetry and portraiture, she was depicted as a virgin or a goddess or both, not as a normal woman. At first, only Elizabeth made a virtue of her virginity: in 1559, she told the Commons, 'And, in the end, this shall be for me sufficient, that a marble stone shall declare that a queen, having reigned such a time, lived and died a virgin'. Later on, poets and writers took up the theme and turned it into an iconography that exalted Elizabeth. Public tributes to the Virgin by 1578 acted as a coded assertion of opposition to the queen's marriage negotiations with the Duc d'Alençon. Putting a positive spin on her marital status, Elizabeth insisted she was married to her kingdom and subjects, 'under divine protection.'

Whoa!! This was rocking. Too *mucking* fuch! *Exactly* the brainwave I needed at this point. For once I had to be grateful for Sangita's condescension for my sad plight. I now knew exactly what I would do. Forget the bag of Pampers; I would send Sangita a crown! But just so she didn't get swollen-headed and start feeling like a real queen and try to usurp my soon-to-be title I would send her one of Kaveri's Barbie doll plastic princess crowns. A gift plus an insult at the same time – like a backhanded compliment. *Oooh!* This was all suddenly so exciting.

Now I knew exactly how I would spend the next few days/months/years or however long it took me to find a husband. But the first thing I'd do before I did anything else would be to announce my born-again virgin status along with my intention of turning into a nun. So no one had an inkling of what was *really* swishing about in my head.

Like my dreams of becoming the murderous monarch of the morons who were mucking with my brain. (Note: here the word is *murderous* – not *murderer*. Intention is everything. Or at least that's what the new-age spiritual gurus say. What follows is destiny.)

Goodness gracious, great balls of fire – what a fantastic way to vent my ire!

Once Kaveri was old enough I would openly go on a rampage *a la* Phoolan Devi the Bandit Queen– but for now it was vital that I hid my inner animus with outer acuity. Just like Elizabeth of England, the virgin queen. After all, it was no coincidence, was it, that I had been right there when the movies on these legendary queens were being made by my ex husband? Movies that had shot him onto the world stage; simultaneously plunging my pop-star paradise into the abyss of obscurity.

Oh, I had been up-close and personal, reading every line before it was spoken on the big screen. Observing every cadence and nuance; absorbing it all. It's no happenstance that you were there, Suchitra – it's your present life karma. I patted myself on the back. Suddenly I was sorted and knew it all – my past, present and future life. God works in mysterious ways to lead us to our salvation. What goes around comes around; it's the divine law of the universe.

I felt tempted to call Sangita and thank her but restrained myself at the last moment. She would just get another reason to boast. Highly avoidable. I put down my cellphone. What if I blurted out my awesome strategy in my insomniacal euphoria? No, best I say nothing at all. Not to anyone. Actions speak louder than words. Soon the world would be my oyster. I would still go ahead with burning the girlies and Ramu and Amma, *et al*, as per the original plan, but now I would exercise my precious academic genes and do it with ingenuity instead of depending on my 'to-be-husband' to execute the brilliance that had originated from my own head in the first place. It was so typical of men to take credit for all the clever things that happened in the world, *na*? Why give Shekhar the pleasure of saying, 'See it was because you were married to me while I made those movies that you could pull this off and make something of your life instead of just sitting around and complaining that I had ruined your musical ambitions and your chance of having more babies.'

Naah – I would stay mum.

My hooded, stoical eyes would be more powerful than Viagra, rhinoceros horn, even. This time around I excused myself the sexual connotations of my potent-eyes' symbolism. After all, I was not a dumb, idle, aspiring wife playing lotto on television any more. I was a woman with a burning mission-possible – everything is fair in war.

So before I set about setting all those in my life ablaze, I would come up with Machiavellian disguises. I would paint these impersonations myself, on cloth masks. Different faces. A combination of the white paint Queen Elizabeth smeared on her face to disguise her devious conniving core as she ruled her noble kingdom with an iron hand, and the red bandanna that Phoolan Devi wore around her forehead. The massacre bandanna badge.

I would wear different masks every single time; varied permutations and combinations of the same theme. No duplicates, thank you very much. Copies are for the mediocre – not for queens. Like the fake labels that Minty the wannabe socialite wears expecting us to believe they are genuine. She even has the gall to quote the original price (that too, all wrong) when it's so obvious that what she's wearing has been purchased from Lokhandwala market at a hundredth of that. Once, she even forgot to take the price tag off at a massive New

Year's Eve gala and tried to pass off her shoes as Prada. *Uff!* Tackiness personified.

Anyway, coming back to my vendetta plan: After the crime was committed, i.e. I had confined my victims in a room and set it on fire, and just before I let them out, so they wouldn't char and die…(This is what I meant when I said my intentions were *murderous*, but not to *be* a murderer – I am a good girl from a girl family, after all, not some lowlife criminal)…I would escape leaving just enough clues around the scene of the crime. Like make each mask in duplicate and throw the second one to the ground minutes before I exited the crime scene. So that people knew they were dealing with somebody dangerous – lethal even – but never guessed my true identity. I would wear one mask around my face to cover it completely, not even a hair visible, and carry the other in the hip pocket of my thigh-revealing mini skirt, worn over my cleavage-exposing top. This dress code was mainly to spite Amma when many years later my identity would be finally discovered and she would cringe in apologetic shame at my *chaddi choomchee* costume. It would also ensure maximum attention from the media – national and global – and keep myself in the front pages forever. Nothing sells better than nudity. *'Disguise Queen Strikes Again!'* Naah – disguise was too common a word. Make that '*Camouflage Queen*'. Yes, that sounded better – phonetically anyway. I would become the next famous queen after Bandit Queen and the Virgin Queen. And Shekhar would finally realize he should have not ignored me during all those years of our marriage. Not gone around chasing other queens while the grandest of the monarchs lay in waiting for him at home, baking hot, buttered scones.

Sadly, I couldn't start my plan with Shekhar, the very person responsible for this sad and lonely condition of mine.

After all Kaveri needed a daddy, *na*?

'Stop it, Chitty. First you forced him to marry you pretending to be this sweet innocent girl from a good family – and then you forced him to divorce you and shamed your good family. When will you take responsibility for your own actions?'

Right now, right now right now, Amma.

I am taking responsibility for my life right now.

Don't tell me I didn't warn you.

Ha ha ha ha ha!

♋

It wasn't until Kaveri barged into my room at 6 a.m. to get ready for school that I realized I had been up the whole night. And not until she started to scream that I discovered that I had tried out one of my 'Camouflage Queen' disguises. White powder blended with water and applied unevenly on parched tired skin. Dark kohl eyes. And the crowning glory of a red bandanna tied around my forehead. *Oh no!* I had no recall of cutting up my favourite T-shirt up. When had I done that? Kaveri started to cry. So loud it woke up Amma and Nana, snoring in the next room.

'*Aiyyo*, Kaveri darling, what happened to you, ra kanna?'

Luckily, as I had worn the make up with my nightclothes still on, my true disguise was still not fully exposed. So my parents would have no clue that I was the Camouflage Queen when they saw me appear in the papers a few days from now.

I assured them all that I was actually rehearsing for a new role in a musical theatre production that I had agreed to perform in just yesterday.

'What's the play called?' Kaveri asked suspiciously. 'Is it a ghost story?' she stared incredulously at my white powder-smeared face, pulling the red bandana off. 'Mamma, I thought this was your favourite T-shirt. Why did you cut it up?'

I wondered why I had cut it up too.

I had no recall whatsoever of having done it. I would have to wait for next month's alimony cheque to clear in order to afford another expensive one like it again. Dang! Trying to hide my panic and disappointment about that depressing fact, I instead told Kaveri that I was rehearsing for the adaptation of the classic *'How to Marry a Millionaire'*. I had the starring role in it with eight solos to sing!

Her look of disbelief increased.

Now Kaveri has never heard me sing, nor believed that I was a famous pop-star. Even when I'm asked to sign autographs at malls and events, she assumes it's because I used to be her daddy's wife. I even tried showing her some of my videos on YouTube – short skirts so hip and happening and all.

'Is that really you, Mamma?' she would ask uncomfortably. 'Y'all used to dress so weird, *na*, in olden times?'

Olden times?

Just you wait, sweetheart.

Your Mamma's time starts now!

Just to prove to my parents and Kaveri that my camouflage queen disguise was actually for a musical play that I was rehearsing for, I fished out my harmonium and decided to do some singing practice while Kaveri brushed her teeth and got ready for school. I hadn't done this in a decade, my vocal cords were rusty.

'*Sa re ga ma...*' I croaked.

'Mamma, your voice is cracking...'

'*Sa re ga ma...*' I tried again, feeling the constricting noose of failure tighten over my parched throat.

'Mamma, please stop it, you're sounding really weird. At least take your make-up off. Your play is in Hindi?'

'No, baby, it's an English musical. *Do re me...*' I tried belting out again, the noose's grip feeling tighter and tighter.

Try as I might I couldn't go beyond the *me*...

I couldn't breathe any more.

I started to choke and struggle for breath. 'Nothing to worry about, my baby,' I gasped, clutched my pounding heart. 'I'm just preparing for my role. In the play *How to Marry a Millionaire*' my character suffers from anxiety attacks.'

Somehow I managed to convince Kaveri not to scream and bring Amma and Nana back into the room again.

'It's okay, Mamma. Don't cry. I know you're stressed. Everything will be fine. I promise I'll tell Daddy that this Diwali I don't want the iPad 4, okay? I'll ask him to buy you the insomnia oil instead.'

'*Sa re ga ma...Do re me...Sa re re ga ma...Do re me...Do re me.*' I struggled to hear my own voice over the roar in my ribcage.

'Mamma! Stop it! You're scaring me. Mamma, please...'

'No, *you* stop it. Let me rehearse in peace.'

'Don't you love me any more, Mamma?'

'I am not just your mamma. Stop it. Stop going *Mamma Mamma* all the time. I am not just a mother! I am also a person – an artist. But do you care? All you do is laugh at me and put me down! Belittling me all the time! Don't sing! Don't laugh! Don't do this, don't do that. I'm sick of your insults! You are selfish – just like your daddy. Show some respect, understood? Or don't call me Mamma ever again!'

'Why can't I call you Mamma?

'Because I am sick and tired of it. For eleven years all I have done is be your Mamma, given up everything that was ever important to me. And what do I get in return? Mamma, don't do this. Don't wear that. Mamma don't sing, Mamma you're so weird. I'm tired of your rebukes all the time – get that?'

It was official.

I had plunged headlong into an anxiety attack, replete with palpitations, and shortness of breath and a sweeping dizziness.

Weeping hysterically and all – right in the presence of my little, eleven-year-old daughter.

It was Kaveri's turn to burst into tears. She ran out of her room shouting out to her grandparents, 'Amma-ma, Thatha come soon! Something has happened to Mamma! Call the doctor! Quick...'

I collapsed in a heap of hiccupping tears.

It was the second time in the last ten days that I had fainted.

11

Even three days after I regained consciousness the loop around my neck persisted, keeping me locked in a strangled silence.

Not a whisper, not an ooh or aah escaped my lips.

Shrink was summoned.

I resisted, scribbling *No! No! No!* furiously on pieces of scrap and A4 sized paper, gesticulating with my hands and screaming out a silent protest. I didn't want to see Shrink. I wanted to be left alone.

If Shrink arrived in a new upgraded car I would kill her for sure! I pointed to my neck with the index finger of my right hand and made a slicing motion, sticking my tongue out to express my intentions of killing Shrink if I ever saw her face again. I made a perfect dead face – rolling up my eyes, twisting my tongue, lolling my head and all. It scared the living daylights out of my parents. They asked Shrink to come right away. Not tomorrow, or later today, but this moment. As in now! now! *Now!*

Since I was all flipped out and my voice wouldn't emerge in spite of repeated gargling with potassium permanganate, I wrote down my intent on a piece of paper and showed it to Nana. He assured me he would send my car to pick her up, ignoring my next note, to then let me gargle with potassium cyanide rather than potassium permanganate. He hugged me tight. 'You'll be fine, ra chilaka. Don't worry so much. Just relax...'

On arrival, Shrink looked graver, more depressed and infinitely more suicidal than me. Now I knew it was true. Shrinks were the craziest of the lot – they only survived by projecting their insanity onto others. Just as I'd learnt to make insomnia and anxiety candles, because of how much I suffered from both, they'd studied madness to understand their own jig-sawed brain cells. I started plucking at my throat as if to pull out the glass shards that were lodged within. Why didn't everybody just leave me alone? After much pushing away of Shrink with my bare hands and kicking my legs in protest, I agreed to let Shrink address me.

'Suchitra, let's do one thing. You enjoy painting, right? I'll give you five words, and you paint whatever comes into your mind. Don't be afraid. Unleash yourself. You don't even have to show the works to me or anyone else if you don't want to.'

What was this, a bloody exam? Like if you want to be a doctor – do mèdicine! If you want to be a manager – do an MBA. If you want to be a certified psycho – do painting!

Her list was to the point. I had to come up with images for the following words:

1. Myself
2. Mother
3. Marriage
4. Money
5. Music

She gave me five weeks to present my 'am-I-or-am-I-not-a-psycho?' answer-sheet, insisting that I do the paintings strictly in the order prescribed by her.

'The problem seems to be with M,' Shrink purred.

The *letter* M? WTF?

'Mmm…' Nod of the head, scratch of the nose, *long,* twangy, nasal sigh! 'Mmm…If you notice, Mr Krishnamoorthi, all of Suchitra's mental blocks are to words that start with the letter M – mother, meditation, marriage, music – it's why she couldn't go beyond the *sa re ga ma* or the *do re mi.* It seems like she's stuck at M...'

I've lost my voice, Shrink. Not my hearing. Did she think I couldn't hear the bullcrap she was feeding my parents?

Nana looked impressed by her profound prognosis, he sighed.

Amma wept, 'Please, help my daughter, doctor. Such a brilliant child! What has happened to her?'

Shrink's chest puffed with importance. She folded a sniffling Amma into her comforting arms. 'She'll be fine, Aunty. It's my job to ensure that, don't worry!'

Amma's tears froze to an abrupt halt: 'Why are you calling him "Mr Krishnamoorthi" and me "Aunty"? I am *eight* years younger than him!' Amma looked outraged. The age difference between my parents was actually six years, but for some reason Amma always said eight. And she had the gall to ask me why *I* sometimes lied about my age!

'Well, uh, what I meant, Mrs Krishnamoorthi, is that it is vital we unravel the *Maya* – also a word starting with M if you notice – of Suchitra's mind; the intellectual paradigms she has trapped herself in to deal with emotional trauma. So please make sure she does these paintings – and exactly in the order prescribed. It's *vital*.'

Amma's brow creased: 'Maya is illusion. Myth. Are you trying to say my daughter is *mental*?'

'No, no, Mrs Krishnamoorthi. You see, the etymology of Maya in Hindu philosophy is much wider. It means many things – not just illusion. Like meter, measurement, music, mother goddess even –'

'*Really?* Mother goddess?' Amma looked impressed. Highbrow academic bullshit always worked on her even though she often didn't quite understand its meaning. Her eyes responded with wide-eyed gratitude.

Shrink looked relieved and continued hurriedly, 'It's the key to discovering the cosmic connection of our inner and outer universe. It is through Maya that we understand Leela, which, as you know, is the cosmic dance of expression. Divine Play. You see, I try and adopt a holistic rather than clinical approach to my...'

I hurled my pencil at Shrink. She got the message and ran. It was my turn to roll my eyes in gratitude but it didn't last long. My gratitude, that is. Full-throttled rage took over in minutes leaving me gasping and choking all over again.

No sooner had Shrink left than I was plied with canvases and paints and brushes and tearful pleas to at least give it a try. I agreed on one condition. I wrote my terms down very clearly with the same pencil I had hurled at Shrink a few minutes ago. No one – *no one* (with the exception of Kaveri, of course) was to disturb me for five whole weeks. No phone calls, no visitors, no barging into my room to ask me if I'd eaten, or slept, or shat. No knocking at my door, either.

When I needed food I would ring the bell for the cook, and I would *not* eat the food prepared by Amma – *no* way! She had to stay out of the kitchen. Amma looked suitably hurt but what else did she expect? Did she think I was such a dolt? The minute Amma knew she had free rein she would insult and fire my staff so that by the time I emerged from my self-imposed, five-week exile I would find that my cook, driver, maid and everybody else had run away, stealing all my valuable crystal, rugs and towels. I would then be running around to maid agencies and begging friends and neighbours to find me suitable replacements; posting my requirements on Facebook, my Blackberry messenger status and even my blog. *'Urgently needed cook, driver, maid – no experience required. Salary no bar – desperate. Please help!' Uff!* So, yes, it was absolutely imperative that Amma stay out of my kitchen – and give Kaveri vitamin syrup for her perceived nutritional deficiencies, caused by her false impression of my laziness and disregard for my own child's growing needs.

For once in my life I got my way without sparring.

Here's what I came up with – it didn't take me five weeks. It took me five days – actually fifteen – the first ten of which I did nothing except loll around on my bed, binge on pizzas, and zombie out in front of the idiot box.

I emerged out of my room only to check that Amma was following my instructions and not cooking while I wasn't watching, and my staff hadn't all run away already.

Kaveri came in every day after school to ask me if I was all right. I held her close and assured her I was.

'I don't care what anybody says. You're the best Mamma in the world.' It was the teasing of a classmate in school that her mom had gone psycho that had prompted the sudden assurance.

'Thank you, my baby,' I hugged her ferociously, struggling to swallow the boulder-sized lump in my throat.

In the next five days I painted in a torrent of tears – it all came pouring out. Amma, Nana, Kaveri, they all left me alone. I forgot the passage of time and worked day and night, splashing colour on canvas – letting myself go.

Maya, Leela or whatever blah – it all poured out of my amygdala.

Note: The amygdala (Latin, corpus amygdaloideum) is an almond-shaped set of neurons located deep in the brain's medial temporal lobe; known to play a key role in the processing of emotions, the amygdala forms part of the limbic system. In humans and other animals, this subcortical brain structure is linked to both fear responses and pleasure. Its size is positively correlated with aggressive behaviour across species. In humans, it is the most sexually-dimorphic brain structure, and shrinks by more than 30% in males upon castration.

Conditions such as anxiety, autism, depression, post-traumatic stress disorder, and phobias are suspected of being linked to abnormal functioning of the amygdala, owing to damage, developmental problems, or neurotransmitter imbalance.

MYSELF

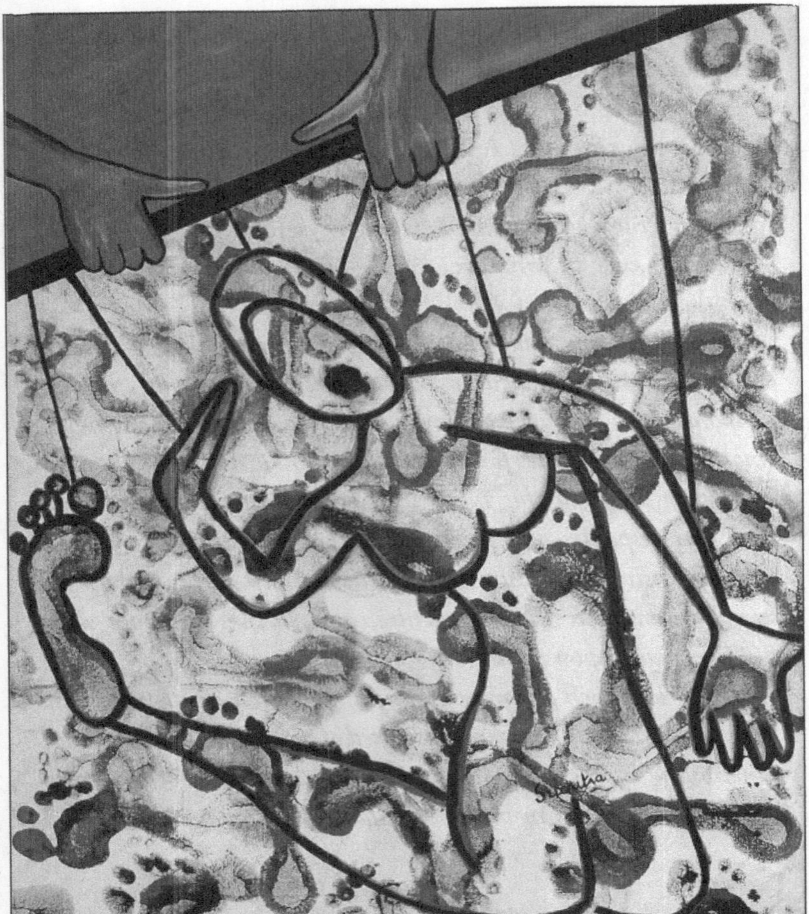

MOTHER

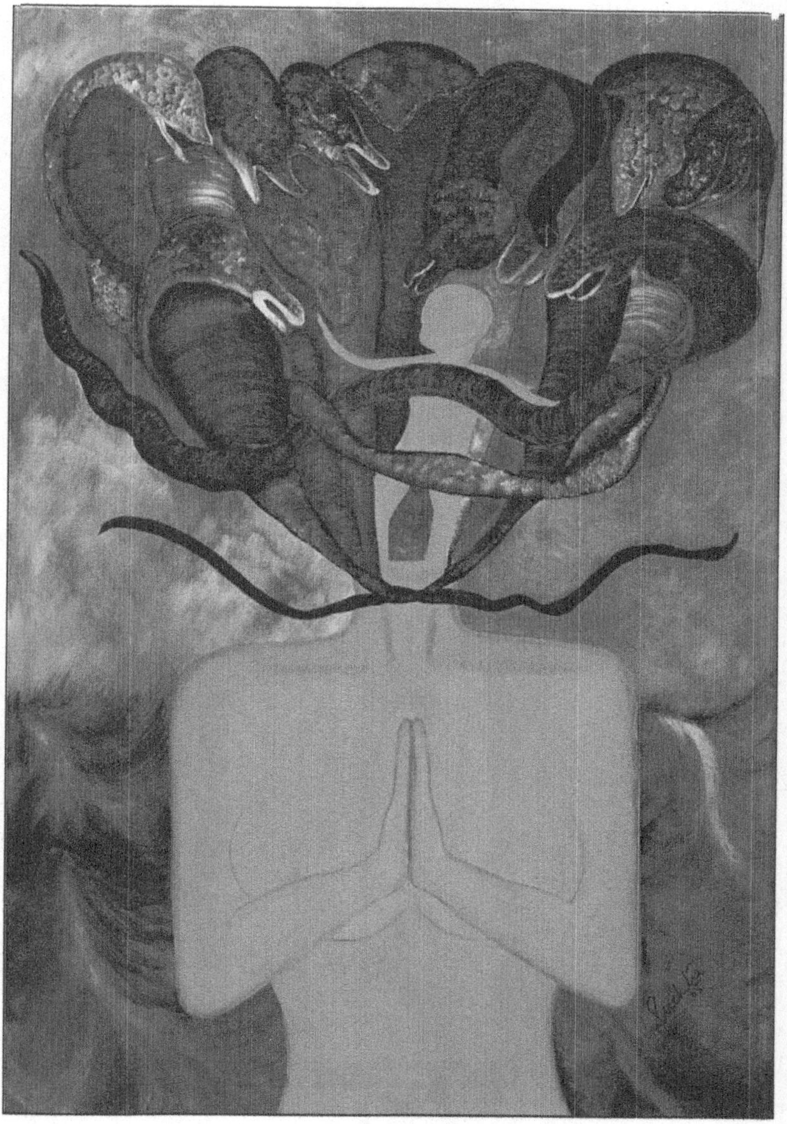

MARRIAGE

MONEY

MUSIC

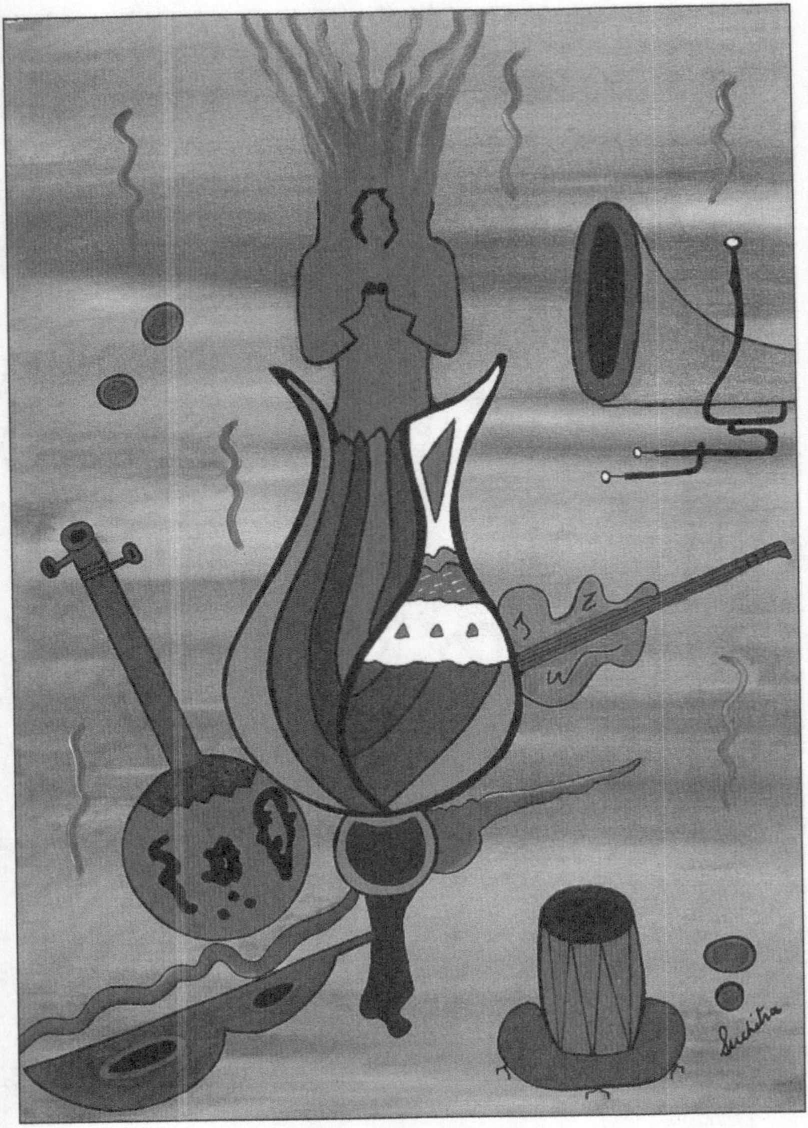

At the end of five days I hurled down my brush and heaved a sigh of relief.

♋

Amma cried and whimpered.

Nana kissed my forehead and thumped my back. 'Well done, ra chilaka.'

Shekhar pursed his lips and let out a slow whistle. '*Phew!* That's a relief. At least now I know it's not my fault. It's your mother's. Ha ha.'

That made Amma bawl even more

'Is this the way you see your mother? Why are you always trying to malign me when all I have ever done is live for my children? After all the sacrifices I have made? How would you react if Kaveri thought the same way about you?'

'This is not about you, Amma; this is about *me*. My art is how I feel – nothing to do with anybody else.'

'What do you mean "nothing to do with anybody else"? Then why have you called it "Mother"? Just because you are frustrated it doesn't mean it's my fault. Nana, let us go back to Bangalore immediately. I have not come here to be insulted. After all that I have done for my children…'

Shrink stared hard and deep and took prolific notes, tapping her nose and twirling a strand of excessively coloured hair. '*Hmm…*' she went. '*Hmm…* see, pain and paint are practically the same word – just an alphabet more… *Hmm.*'

She looked closely at my paintings and then grandly announced: 'Suchitra's next set of paintings will be based on words starting with the letter P…' Her voice was smug; obviously pleased with her progress in unravelling my Maya so far.

Amma, reluctant to concur with her recommendation and

afraid of what further pain to her my paintings with the letter p would bring, glanced at Shrink's notes. Her eyes widened in horror as she read on further:

'"P for: Paranoid Schizophrenia. It is a schizophrenia subtype in which the patient has false beliefs (delusions) that somebody or some people are plotting against them.

'(Note:- *Suchitra thinks all her problems are her Amma's, ex husband's or mine i.e. her shrink's fault. May need medication since reacting badly to vocational-skills training.)*

'People with paranoid schizophrenia, as with most subtypes may also have auditory hallucinations – they hear things that are not real. The individual may also have delusions of personal grandeur – a false belief that they are much greater and more powerful and influential than they really are. An individual with paranoid schizophrenia may spend an extraordinary amount of time thinking of ways to protect themselves from their persecutors.

'(Note:- *Suchitra's belief that she could burn her imagined enemies and get away with it is an alarming predicament indeed. Try ECT – Electroconvulsive therapy.)*

"Nevertheless, paranoid schizophrenia is a chronic (long-term, lifelong) condition which may eventually lead to complications, including suicidal thoughts and behaviour. It is the most common schizophrenia type. **Paranoid schizophrenia** is *schizophrenia characterized predominantly by delusions of persecution and megalomania*

'(Note:- *Suchitra's asinine plan of turning herself into the "Camouflage Queen" is a frightening example or how deep the disease has spread. May require hospitalization.)'*

Amma snatched the sheaf of papers from Shrinks hands and tore them to bits.

'ECT? Hospitalization? My Chittu is not mental! You are! M for Mental! P for Pathetic! That's what you are – a pathetic mental case who is just fleecing my daughter! Get out. *Po veh,* charlatan!'

(*Po Veh* is 'Get out' in Telugu, and charlatan is quack – or is it? Oh no, why was my brain getting all cloudy again?)

'I will handle this, ra Chittappa,' Amma assured me, burning holes into Shrink's eyes with her angry gaze. '*Po!* Get out! Just now! Before I call the P for Police! Paranoid schizophrenia – how *dare* you?'

'No, no, Mrs Krishnamoorthi,' Shrink neighed, trying to pull the reins of Amma's rage back in control, before she tore out her hair as she had her notes. So that her greedy 'make truckloads of money from proving other people are mad before they expose your crazy sick ass themselves' coffers remained greased forever. 'Erm...Please don't take any of this personally, Aunty.'

'*Aunty*?! Why are you calling me *Aunty* again? Don't you have any shame? You are not that young, you know. By your age I was already a grandmother. M for Moron.'

Whoooaaa! I had to concede my Amma was a star!

She reminded me of the times she would shoo revellers away from our door during the Holi festival. It was the only time I didn't object to her strict ways as I always hated all that icky, sticky water and colour myself. Amma would just stand there and glare – and no one dared utter a word or anoint her forehead with colour, like they forcibly did to all the other neighbours who refused to come down and play. They would just smile and scoot, 'Uh, tell Suchitra we just came to say Happy Holi, Aunty.'

'Sorry, Mrs Krishnamoorthi,' Shrink said, hastily. 'The "Aunty" just slipped out. And of course I have shame; which is why it's my moral duty to educate you on what is going on. The etiology of Suchitra's state of mind has nothing to do with you and the wonderful mother you are, have been, and will continue to be for as long as you live. You see, it's only Suchitra's false sense of frustrated persecution and inability to take stock of her own failure that is putting you at fault.'

My god! Was I paying Shrink to degrade me like this? What did she think, that I was *deaf*?

I had lost my voice – not my hearing. And that, too, was a thing of the past. With every stroke of the brush my voice had become stronger and stronger. Couldn't she *hear* that? This was too much. Way, *way*, too much. To think and accept the sad truth that even women of affluence and science such as Shrink – and not just illiterate masseuses such as Indu – turn into subservient sycophants under the threat of imminent slaps (from the absolutism of the Amma's of the world), and the loss of livelihood, was more than my fragile heart could handle. I was learning my lessons in the hardest way imaginable.

In my defence, Amma forgot about her own feelings of vilification and shooed Shrink out the door. She looked ready to strike, wagging her open palm dangerously in front of Shrink's cheek:

'*If* I *ever* see you again...*Po!* Get out!' Amma warned. 'Pathetic Mental case. "P" and "M", my foot!'

'Thank you, Amma,' I whimpered after Shrink had left.

'No need to thank me,' Amma sniffed. 'I was just doing my duty as a mother. That shrink of yours is dangerous and you better stay away from her. You need to work, that's all. There is nothing wrong with you.' She handed me a fresh canvas and paints and sniffed some more. 'Why don't you do some more painting, ra kanna? Forget about everything else. We are here to look after Kaveri. You have nothing to worry about.'

'Should I paint in the same order as before? And what if you get upset again?' Was this some kind of trick? Like, 'Please come back home, ra kanna but as soon as you do, I'm going to ask you to get out the minute you get up my nose again.'

Amma's eyes clouded with unshed tears. 'No, ra kanna, it's not a trick. I know you have always thought I was too strict and that all your problems are my fault. But I wish I had been stricter and never allowed you to marry Shekhar, then none of this would have ever happened.'

Great. Everybody play the blame game. Absolve yourself, pass the buck, and choke me to death with your selective amnesia.

'If Mamma didn't marry Daddy how would I have been born?' Kaveri refused to be let out of the big fat family drama. Oh no, I hadn't even noticed her enter.

'Please leave the room, baby. We are talking big people things.'

'Mamma, you don't love me, or what? Is that why you're always asking me to go out? And is that why Ammama Thatha says I shouldn't disturb you when you're painting or sitting on the computer the whole day?'

'Didn't I tell you *not* to stop Kaveri from entering my room?' I yelled at Amma. Why couldn't my parents ever respect my wishes? I didn't realize I had shouted aloud till I heard Kaveri cry, 'Why are you screaming, Mamma? Daddy's right. You're always screaming.'

'Did Daddy really say that? Well if I start to tell you about all the things your Daddy does…'

'*Aiyyo,* stop it, Chitappa. Not in front of Kaveri…'

But it was too late. There was no stopping the ensuing weep-fest. Luckily, Amma allowed Kaveri to cry louder than herself, which was a sure sign that things were a-changing. I had never had that good luck or privilege.

'Nana – book our tickets back to Bangalore. We don't need to waste any more time here and keep listening to her snubs...'

Dang! I didn't want my parents to leave yet. Because all this frenzied painting – even though I hadn't realized it earlier – had actually cleared my mind considerably. I no longer felt like a scrambled egghead, more like a rough-edged omelette. Thoughts of launching my new career as Camouflage Queen had abated. Though, I still intended to sue Shrink. And burn her too. But that was *after* I took my desperately-needed vacation. And since the only way I could take that desperately-needed vacation was by persuading my parents to stay back and look after Kaveri while I was away, I decided it was best to appease Amma.

'That was the initial burst, Amma. In a few days I will show you my new set of paintings. Then you'll see that I am actually shedding my negative thoughts.'

'You can *never* shed your negative thoughts. This is too much – Nana, please book our tickets immediately.'

But this time around I wasn't about to let them go easily. The liberty to remain locked in my room and ignore all Mamma/Dog owner/Domestic Slave responsibilities and worries was a freedom I hadn't experienced in the longest time. Not since Kaveri had been born and motherhood had laid its claims on every living cell of my being. I was desperate to stretch it for just a few days more. I had a plan in mind, too – to take up Pankaj on his holiday offer. A vacation would do me good. Very good indeed.

'I cannot rest until I return to my own home,' Amma snapped. 'After all that I have sacrificed for my children...what does that "Mother" painting mean, *haan*? And that too, did she have to paint the body *naked*? Shameless!'

I appealed to Nana with my eyes. 'Please, please, *please,* Nana. Stay a few days more?'

It seemed like he got the message. Not the 'me-going-on-a-wannabe-sex-romp' intention but just the 'please-Nana-don't-go-please'.

'We'll discuss it tomorrow, Sulochi,' Nana said and guided Amma to their room firmly by the shoulders. 'We can all do with some rest now.'

Amma didn't argue.

Whoo hoo! My Daddy strongest!

I had rarely ever seen my parents touch. In fact, for the longest time, I had argued with my classmates in school, saying that it was impossible that I had been born *that* way. I imagined I had been created by a wave of god's magic wand – much like Jesus. I got a migraine in every class that taught us about the birds and the bees. But still, it was better than my classmate, Debbie. The first time she'd learnt that she might have come into the world by the corrupt concept of coitus she had consumed an entire bottle of blue Camlin ink, leaving a trickle to drip down the side of her lip like vampire blood, and banging her head on the school desk shouted, 'Let me die, let me die!' She had been utterly distraught. 'My parents are not like that! Teacher is telling a lie!'

I shuddered to think of where she was now or what kind of paintings she would possibly churn out if asked to. The nuns in my all girls' convent school had made it worse.

'Don't stand in the balcony when there is a breeze,' they warned.

'What do you mean by that, Sister? I live in a sea-facing flat opposite an open park. It's always breezy…'

'Don't try to act so innocent, Suchitra. You know *exactly* what I mean. When the wind is blowing hard is when all the boys come out. So, if you have to stand in the balcony make sure you are always in jeans, understood? Or hold your skirt tight against your thighs so it doesn't fly!'

Had Amma trained Sister Pereira in the *chaddi choomchee* philosophy, or what? Or was it the other way around?

Just to make sure my parents didn't slip away and I could revel in a few days more of worry-free angst-ridding, I hid Nana's wallet. Why take a chance? The next morning when Nana's wallet theft was discovered I feigned ignorance and pretended to look for it alongside them.

'*Aiyyo*, let us report it to the police, Nana,' Amma panicked. 'Maybe that Shrink has stolen it. She's a greedy creature after all – mental case! No wonder she was trying to butter me up so much.'

Nana didn't want any hassle with the cops. 'It's a sign that Chittu needs us to stay,' he said benignly, squinting a hard long look at my guilty eyes. I quickly averted my gaze, relieved when he flicked a quick wink at me. I would return the wallet soon. Cross my heart and swear on my god.

The phallus-symboled one, of course.

My plan went smoothly. Pankaj said he would make the arrangements at a spa in Bangkok. 'Erm... what *kind* of booking?'

He told me not to worry because he was tied up in a business negotiation and wouldn't be able to make time anytime soon, so I was on my own. That was a relief. I promised to reimburse him. He agreed but insisted we would discuss it later.

In the few days prior to departure I made a fresh series of paintings, mostly to assure Amma that I loved her and I was indeed in the process of shedding my negative thoughts. But more than that to calm her down and make sure my home ran smoothly while I was away. The marriage painting made Kaveri happy too, she hugged me tight. All was well in her world again.

MOTHER:

Note: See Amma – I love you and I understand that you love me too. Let's hug and make up shall we?

Note: Marriage is for companionship and bringing more beautiful babies into the world just like Kaveri. Who said anything about sex?

MONEY

Note: Money earned through intelligence and modest conduct is the ultimate jewel in the Indian womans crown (please note poetry on veil.) Lesson learnt: will never waste poetry on illiterate greedy essential oil merchants ever again

MYSELF

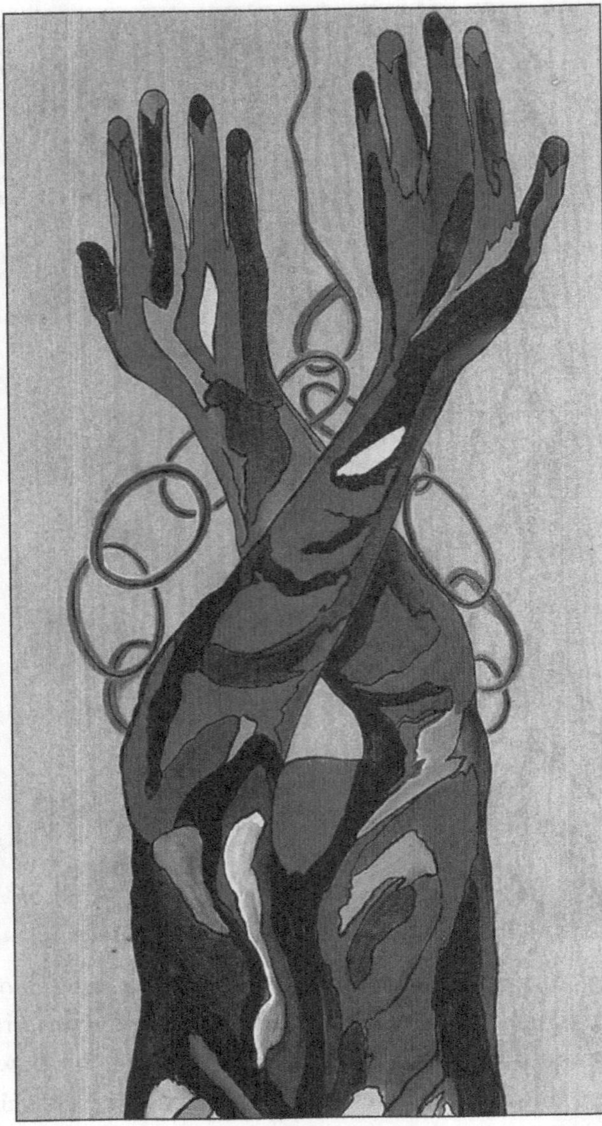

'Look at your painting of yourself – you're tying up your own hands. Only you can free them. Just tell your parents you are going to Bangkok. What's the big deal? Grow up.'

Shut up. How could I? The fact that I had even considered going with Pankaj made me feel like a slut already. So I told Amma that I was taking off to Chandni's farmhouse in Alibaug, refusing Nana's offer to drop me there. I told him it was best I take Chandni's car since her driver knew the way there and all.

As I was leaving Kaveri made me a little card. I clutched it in my palm for solace –

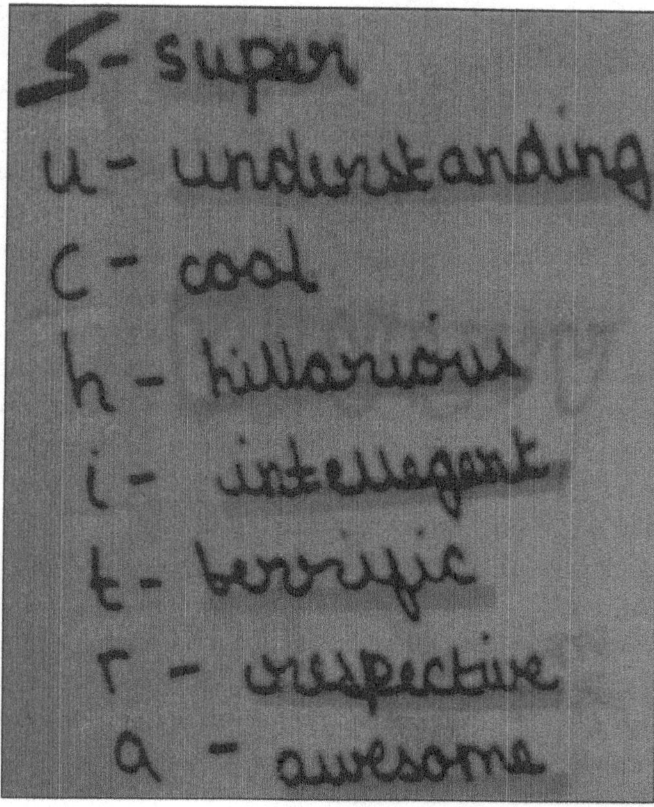

Nana called me three times even before I entered the aircraft. 'What is all that noise? Why does it sound like you are at an airport?'

'Oh, uh Chandni is going to Bangkok, so I just came to drop her off at the airport,' I replied.

I then called Chandni to tell her not to go anywhere that my parents were likely to bump into her. That was easy to manage – Amma didn't do Gucci and Chandni didn't do Muthulaxmi. But when I asked Chandni in the same breath to keep checking and seeing that Kaveri was all right and that my staff had not been scolded away, she protested. She was no James Bond. She couldn't hide *and* spy at the same time now, could she?

'Relax, Suchitra. Chill. Everything will be fine, just enjoy your holiday, and make sure you are back for my karva chauth party, okay? I've made some amazing arrangements this time – chocolate and rose mehndi along with the regular henna tattoos. It's our fifteenth, *na*? Imagine, it's been so long. Sometimes I feel like Sanjit and I just got married yesterday.'

'Erm, okay, girlfriend. Sure, thanks. I love you too.'

I slept through takeoff and landing, waking up to my ringing telephone as the aircraft taxied into Bangkok's Suvarnabumi airport. 'Why weren't you picking up your phone? We got worried. You've reached safely, no?'

'I'm fine, Nana. My battery died, that's all.'

'And what is that strange ring tone? Sounds Chinese or something.'

Oops, why hadn't I thought about that? Dang!

'I told you, Nana. Chandni's gone to Bangkok – that's why I dropped her off at the airport. I think our phones got swapped by mistake or something...'

'*Aiyyo,* Chittu, what are you saying, ra kanna? Are you sure you'll be all right alone? Have you been drinking wine again?'

Uff! My parents drove me knucking futs! 'Yes I've had two whole bottles already *and* I'm going to have sex too! Any problem?'

'Okay, ra chilaka, Relax. Don't get upset. Enjoy yourself. I just got worried when you didn't pick up the phone, that's all…'

I stumbled through Immigration, reeling under the daze of yet another attack of Boxer's Syndrome and jet lag, and bumped straight into Pankaj at the baggage belt.

12

'*Such?*

That unmistakable, lilting caress. No one else could call my name like that. I felt a sudden warmth on my cheek. *Surprise!*

'My flight just landed from Paris,' he smiled tentatively. 'My meeting here got arranged suddenly.'

'Really? Wow! What a coincidence.'

'Yes, it is, and BTW you're looking lovely.'

I jumped into Pankaj's arms just like I had always imagined. Without having to fake a broken toenail. I didn't care that my skirt rode up my waist either – this was Bangkok. In tha tha Thigh land – no shame in being a *chaddi choomchee* here.

He wasn't as strong as sweet-dish Sidharth and my weight had gone up considerably since then. We toppled over the bags and grinned and giggled, oblivious to the world around us. Rising only when the hovering figure of the man carrying Pankaj's name on a little placard refused to move away. Six Senses Spa – *that's* where we were headed? OMG. I gulped

'Yes, it's about an hour's ride,' I was informed as we were ushered into the private plane that would ferry us to the resort and seated ourselves in its plush seats.

In spite of my *chaddi choomchee* exuberance a few minutes before, I now oscillated wildly between exultation and panic, the moral preachings of a lifetime drowning my skull. To what depths had I fallen to be alone in a strange country with a man not wedded to me? But had I known that Pankaj would be there I would have refused his offer – or, would I have? *Dang!* I was no longer sure...and my worry right now, besides the wickedness of my fallen morals, was something else altogether.

While it was true that I was grateful for this vacation opportunity Pankaj had offered – considering I was ready to even go and stay in a slum in Dharavi just to get away from Amma's nagging – I should have asked for some more details before insisting so vehemently that I would pay for this trip, and not been persuaded by his suggestion that we would discuss it later. That way I could have changed the venue to one more suitable to my budget.

If any of you know the *per diem* rates at the Six Senses resorts worldwide you would totally understand my worry. Standing in a mile-long queue in Dharavi to collect water for my daily ablutions was a less frightful prospect than having to cough up for this holiday. And pay I would – no slutty free holidays for me, thank you very much. I'm a good girl I am. Amma would be proud. But how could I possibly achieve that without robbing a bank or something? I fretted and chewed my nails to the bone. 'Do you know nails are a good source of calcium? And since the DNA is the same as our bodies, the absorption into the bloodstream is much higher than through other sources like pills and syrups.'

'Really?' Pankaj smiled.

'Oh, absolutely.' (Intellectual projection was the need of the moment.) 'So the next time you cut your nails, don't throw them away. Remember, it's better to just eat them.'

I had to somehow stop him from noticing my tumbling fall down the precarious steps of depravity. My forced smile quivered with excessive effort, as I jerked my skirt over my knees. My attempts at concealing my nervousness were obviously failing. Pankaj didn't look convinced about my calcium nonsense either. I had to come up with something else soon. *But what?*

'Relax. You'll love this place,' Pankaj smiled, glancing through the file in his hands.

Oh sure I would love it, my best hugger in the world, my worry is something else altogether.

He gently pulled my nervous fingers out of my mouth. It made me almost leap out of my seat, shatter the glass with my fist, and dive outside the window into the calm china blue sky. I had never been skydiving either; perhaps this was my chance.

'It's just that small aircraft get me uncomfortable,' I cleared my throat pretending I had a cough coming on. 'I prefer big aircraft and the service of first-class,' I bragged ridiculously, just so he didn't think I was some impoverished wannabe who had no clue of the high life.

Talking about first-class reminded me I had one other plausible option. I decided I would call up Shekhar on the second-last day of the holiday and tell him I had been kidnapped in Bangkok and ask him to pay the tariff as ransom. Shekhar would have no option other than to pay up. After all, I was the mother of his child, *na*? In that way, Amma was right. Shekhar would always look after me. He had no choice.

Phew. I felt a bit better already. Now that I had come up with my UGG plan to pay for my pleasure I relaxed a bit, controlling the demonic urge to jump off my seat and hug Pankaj tight. Never had a lap looked more inviting.

'Why don't you just relax? How's the painting coming along?'

Wait a minute! How did he know about my recent spurt of paintings? Pankaj had bought several of my paintings over the last years, even commissioning me to make a few on order for his office in Mumbai. Unlike many others who give you the run around when it is time to cough up the cash, his cheques had arrived even before the works had reached him or I had envisioned them.

But I hadn't wielded the paintbrush in over a year, even cancelling exhibition bookings, because I couldn't muster up the energy to do anything but try and get a few hours rest in between all my grab-a-husband schemes. That had been top of mind; everything else could wait.

So Pankaj suddenly asking me about my recent paintings out of the blue made me a bit apprehensive. *Did he think I was psycho too?*

I pressed my head against the plane window trying to keep my eyes on the enchanting view outside, thinking of suitable, sidetracking, subterfuge strategies to evade his queries. Another word starting with P asked by a person whose name also started with a P. I felt the roar creep back into my ears, the window pane starting to invert exactly the same way it had done in the Om Harmonics' class. My heart beat revved a few notches 'How's Amrita?' I squawked.

'She's fine. Just relax. I need some paintings for my new apartment in Bangkok, which is why I asked you.'

'Is Amrita going to be here too, to help you get your house done up?' I knew the tricks married men employed; I wasn't about to fall for this one so easily. Nothing could tempt me into sin.

'No, Amrita's moved out.'

'Moved out?' The ambiguity of this phrase was classic, cheating married-man jargon. I knew that. Moved out, not working out, sorting things out… Naah, I wasn't going to fall prey so easily.

'Have you been to Bangkok before?

'Oh many times – for shopping,' I fumbled on in a bid to uphold my 'I'm-not-a-slutty-impoverished-wannabe' image. 'I love Bangkok. I love travelling, you know.' I rattled of the names of several more destinations around the globe, 'Ischia, Capri, Bahamas and Barcelona – I love em all,' I said mispronouncing several along the way. 'Of course, you know, being a well-heeled international jetsetter – like me, ha ha – Asia is always better than Europe for shopping sprees. And there's no place like Bangkok; which is why me and my girlfriends come here so often.'

Now Pankaj looked bemused. I was beyond noticing. 'Shopping weekends are such fun – but you guys don't do that, *na*? It's a very chick thing.' I wasn't going to make the same mistake I had made with my other prospective husbands and reveal anything about the Stanford university survey. That was my secret weapon; best concealed.

The truth was that I had been to Bangkok just once before – with my sister Sunita. On free tickets won on a club membership she had recently acquired. We had stayed at a modest hotel provided as part of the free deal, and spent all our days roaming around in tuktuks and indulging in some glorious street shopping.

'Yeah, Bangkok's great for shopping,' Pankaj agreed

In spite of the blood pounding in my ears I felt a spasm

of comfort. It was a god-send for Pankaj to have mentioned my paintings at this moment. Now I didn't have to fret about executing my ransom demand plan with Shekhar or come up with a suitable disguise to rob a bank. I would just figure out exactly how much the bill was and gift Pankaj some paintings; would have to make him some more new ones, of course; couldn't possibly give any from my first psychiatric-ward batch of a few days ago.

If Pankaj discovered what exactly was going on in my head he would probably run too, just like all those others I intended to set on fire for the epic humiliation of my turned-down marriage proposals. Besides, who would put those paintings in their home? They belonged more on the walls of the horror art museum.

The paintings that had made Amma weep and Shrink come up with her paranoid schizophrenia diagnosis. Shrink had the gall. *Bitch!* While I had almost forgiven everybody else I would sue her for sure. I would contact my lawyer as soon as I returned to Mumbai – maybe even call him the moment I landed at the resort just so it didn't slip out of my mind.

But wait a minute. Did Shrink's analysis make sense after all? The fact that I was on a holiday seated in a **P**rivate **P**lane with **P**ankaj and he was talking about **M**y **P**aintings got me thinking about the letters **M** and **P** again. Of words like Mohan and *puchak puchak* and *muah* and *penis* and... *Chheh! Shameless! Stop it, Chitty. Move away from such puerile thoughts and don't let this opportunity slip away from your hands. Behave like a bride not a bimbette.*

'Oh, I've had a good run last few weeks. Made a *lot* of paintings. I'll email the images to you – see what you like.'

Trying to sound as cucumber-cool and artistic as possible, I grabbed a sandwich and started to chomp on it furiously, avoiding glancing Pankaj's way. Eye contact with him was warming my cheeks and weirding up my insides.

Breathe in, breathe out, Suchitra. Round your lips into an O, roll your tongue to the top of your mouth, and inhale and exhale again and again. Make sure the sandwich doesn't get stuck in your teeth – *that* is vital. Take another deep breath and form a larger O with your lips to take in larger gulps of air.

Shoot! It was not until I noticed Pankaj staring at me peculiarly that I realized I was actually doing it and not just thinking it in my mind. OMG – did he see my gesture as propositioning him? Like offering him a blow job or something? Yikes!

I quickly spat out the sandwich and muttered through my tightly pursed lips: 'Gosh – why does this taste like peanut butter? I hope it's not. You know I have arachibutyrophobia.'

'You have your own room. You don't have to be so worried.'

Obviously, I have to have my own room. I wouldn't have it any other way. What kind of a girl did he I was? 'Look it's very nice of you to have made this offer but if I had known…'

'My meeting got fixed at the last minute in Bangkok. *Seriously.*'

'And I'm serious too about the arachibutyrophobia thingy. Kaveri has it too. You know what that is, right?'

He said he didn't have the faintest idea.

'It's the fear of peanut butter sticking to the roof of your mouth.'

This part wasn't a lie. Strange as it may sound to the layman such a neurosis does indeed exist. What I didn't mention of course is that Kaveri had developed this revulsion only after I had attended one of her concerts in school with large gashes of peanut butter wedged between my teeth. I myself had never understood her staunch refusal to eat any more peanut butter sandwiches, or her sudden irrational fear of the food item she had once loved till that day. I had discovered it only a few months later when I'd attended the next parent teacher meeting and saw the photographs displayed on her classroom wall. A close-up view of my white-interspersed-with-brown shining peanut-butter coated teeth, grinning alongside other proud parents of her class. None of whom had any ghastly grizzlies protruding from their mouths.

Oh no! Why couldn't my baby have just *told* me of her shame? I would have insisted the teacher take the photograph down rather than having spent a week on internet research trying to figure out children's sudden mood swings and phobias *vis a vis* food, and explained to Kaveri that I had not done it deliberately. I had attended that school concert after a particularly agonizing, week-long bout of insomnia and didn't really know what I was doing. That morning, in fact, I had even rushed back home halfway through the car ride to school when I'd realized I hadn't remembered to change out of my satin night-gown into something more appropriate for a grade 5 school concert.

'Suchitra, please take it easy. You don't have to do anything you don't want to do. and I don't think you're cheap because…'

'Because what?' Discomfort makes the voice aggressive sometimes. The words slammed out my lips like a slap.

'Because you were so happy to see me at the airport.'

Oh no, why was he talking about that? It had been out of

character. I shouldn't have pounced on him like that. I started to feel dizzy and on the verge of another anxiety attack.

'Such, calm down. Why don't you just allow yourself a good time?'

It was the tone of the 'Such' that did it. *Sigh!* How could I resist? I tried to pull my head back together. It was impossible for me to trust any man ever again but I had to give it a try if I wanted to extricate myself out of the cesspool of my current state of woes and live my life happily ever after in a piously wedded, holy matrimonial state. Besides, Pankaj had worked hard to earn his place in my otherwise cluttered shelf, filled with fears, phobias and other assorted psycho knick-knacks. It was very good of him. And now that I knew he didn't think me cheap, and the matter of the bill settlement was resolved, and Amrita was moving out too, I would wait for an opportune moment and propose marriage to him. ASAP.

By the end of this holiday I intended to have a husband and soon we would plan the baby too. It was all going to work out.

I sucked in my breath and thanked the Lord silently. *Om shanti shantee tee hee hee hee.*

♋

The aircraft taxied into the airstrip a short boat ride away from the spa. The salty air swept through my hair like a balm to soothe my nerves, lulling me into a hazy, delicious calm. I smiled and giggled and thanked Pankaj as he led me to my room and agreed to meet him for dinner later after a quick freshen up. I unpacked my bags – refusing the help of the personal Man Friday assigned to each room, delighting in the mating croaks of the peacocks and the sound of the water lapping in the swimming pool outside my villa.

The fact that each villa had its own attached swimming pool to ensure privacy, was a blessing. Unlike the last time I had taken off on a holiday to Goa soon after my divorce. Where children and other assorted uncles and aunties had hovered around asking me if I was the famous Indian actor Rani Mukherjee; even insisting I pose for photographs and sign autographs as her, in spite of my denial. And then, when one leery, middle-aged, pot-bellied kind had almost assaulted me in the pool with, 'I now know who you are. You are not Rani Mukherjee. You are Shekhar Kapur's wife, right?' I had hurried out of the pool and checked out of the hotel, pronto. My identity crisis those days had bordered on the acute. I was ready to plunge a knife into anybody who referred to me as that ever again.

The rarefied air was still and quiet. Amma was so wrong about Pankaj, just as she was about my need to work and so many other things. I wondered about the right time to propose. Should I do it right away, at dinner tonight? Or should I play it by ear and see how it went? Once I got married I wouldn't have to fret about a thing. I would be ensconced in luxury and could live happily-ever-after in his strong, secure, gloriously rich arms. Forget about struggling to buy a bottle of insomnia oil – I could buy the whole plantation!

This was all working out. A few minutes of shut-eye was all that was required to brace myself for the momentous, life-changing night ahead. I was sorted. From Krishnamoorthi to *Ganatra* Whoaaa! *'Doo be doo be doo'* I hummed, *a la* Frank Sinatra. I took out my light pink gown and smoothed it down on the bed beside me. A few minutes of REM sleep and I would set out to conquer my new husband.

When my eyes opened it was already broad daylight. I glanced at the gown I had laid out on the couch in dismay. Oh no! Had I missed dinner? Not that I minded having skipped a meal but I cursed myself on the lost opportunity. Dang! I dressed hurriedly, tripping over the note Pankaj had slipped under my door as I dashed out of my room. *'Hope you had a good rest. Had to leave on some urgent business. Will call you. See you soon.'*

Shoot! I had let the chance of a lifetime slip out of my hands. How could I have slept through such a potentially promising night?

Swallowing my disappointment and resisting the urge to consume an entire box of chocolate that lay by the bedside table (wobbly tummies are detrimental to husband seduction) I decided to make the most of my time at the spa. Massages, swims, and gourmet meals. Some more massages, lounging in the pool, and then some more massages and some more gourmet cuisine.

I could feel the volume of static in my head gradually whittle down to low. As soon as I reached Mumbai I would call Chandni and tell her that the hum in my head has nothing to do with sex, the lack of sex, or her 'how-can-you-survive- without-sex' blah. It had come down on its own accord without me following her puerile suggestions, hadn't it? I just needed to find a husband, chill out a bit, and that's exactly where I was headed.

I would also explain to her that it was high time she stopped being so dumb. Considering she was about to celebrate her fifteenth wedding anniversary and I was again on the threshold of…no, no best not to reveal my plans to anyone. Not until the wedding card was in the post.

Lounging in the swimming pool like this, here, at the Six Senses Spa in Thailand two straight days in a row, no one in sight except the boats in the sea and the palm trees by the villa, was sheer bliss.

Trees and walls make great neighbours. One can always talk to them freely with no risk of them carrying tales and gossiping with other girlfriend trees. No need to fret about anybody watching or listening in, or clicking pictures on their mobile phone just when the PMS cellulite was erupting to an all-time high. And then, to your further horror, to find yourself on strangers' Facebook walls and status updates, on precisely those horribly low self-worth days that you Google yourself for the consolation that you actually exist outside of the four walls of your own home and aside of mothering responsibilities. Like it had happened on my last trip where the leery gentleman insisted I was Rani Mukherjee and then Facebooked, *'Does anybody remember her name? She acted in that movie with Shahrukh Khan. Shekhar Kapur's wife, right?'*

Ha ha ha. The fact that I could laugh about it now was a good sign.

I closed my eyes and lay my head against the swimming pool wall, feeling the volume of buzzing static quieten to a hum. I felt exquisitely anesthetized with relaxation. All my, 'I'm-so-afraid-of-my-life' murmurs dissipating into the cool blue water. 'No photographs, please,' I told the tallest palm wagging my palm in my most sophisticated movie-star gesture.

'What did you say, Suchitra?'

It's a bird! It's a tree! Was somebody talking to me?

Pankaj stood at the other end of the pool in the shadow of

the fading sun, looking like Tom Cruise in *Top Gun*. I felt my heart soar. 'Me? I didn't say anything. I think it was the palm tree talking.' I pressed my hands against the sides of the pool, thrilled to see him again. A blissful buoyancy creeping into my being. 'Yeah – I'm feeling great, thank you.'

'Do you mind if I join you?'

I pinched myself to know it wasn't a dream, holding back a gasp. Since I had decided it was high time I stepped out of my old-fashioned shoes and joined the sexual revolution I pretended a boldness I did not feel at all. Fighting the urge to duck underwater and hide my body, I instead extended my arm and welcomed him into the pool, my experience as an actress once again coming to the fore. My sophistication could have put Greta Garbo to shame.

We swam in silence, floating on our backs and indulging in idle chit chat. I giggled and heated up like a furnace every time he smiled, our eyes met, or our fingers touched. When I could hold myself back no longer I wrapped my arms around him and lay my head on his shoulder. 'Thank you. Nobody has been so sweet to me for a long time. Thank you for not thinking that I'm a…'

'Shush,' Pankaj placed a finger on my lips to hush me, pushing the wet hair from my brow. 'Having a good time?' He kissed me on the forehead. I nodded. I arched my neck and offered him my lips feeling no awkwardness, no shame, willing myself to emerge out of the prison of my own confinement, whimpering a soft yes. The kiss was tentative at first, deepening as my bewilderment of the pleasure coursing through me washed away the last remaining shards of self doubt.

I entwined my fingers in his hair and pulled him closer, luxuriating in the warmth that enveloped our bodies. A bare-chested, non-breasted body was infinitely more pleasurable than a shirted one. I moaned as hope, fear and passion merged, luxuriating in the delicious sensations that pulsed through me. It had been long since I had allowed myself to feel so vulnerable, my long-paralyzed flesh taking its first tentative steps towards discovering the biology of my own needs. I sighed when he slipped the swimsuit off my shoulder, and tucked my head into his shoulder as he carried me to the bed. Astounded by my avarice and longing as I shuddered in rapture over and over again. I floated high above the stratosphere, our lovemaking a dance choreographed by the gods.

With a surge of new-found confidence I dialled Mumbai the following night. 'Give Kaveri the phone,' I demanded, refusing to answer any of Nana's questions about my well-being and safety. 'And if Amma cooks, tell her that I'll never be her daughter again.'

Now that my husband was almost in my grasp I didn't have to tolerate anything outside my will. As soon as we were married I would tell Pankaj that handling Amma was henceforth his responsibility. I couldn't deal with the pressure any more.

'Relax, chilaka. I hope you are enjoying yourself. Kaveri is sleeping with the night light on and Amma gave her the vitamin syrup an hour ago.'

Kewl! Good parents! Finally!

'Oh, true heaven is a place on earth,' I sang at the top of my voice as I jumped into Pankaj's waiting arms. From famine to feast, from frigid to nympho – my metamorphosis had happened overnight. This was all working out.

UGG – U Go Girl!

Sigh! Oooh! Yum yum!

Rocking!

PART 3

Six months later...My Happily-Ever-After... The Indoctrination of Penultimate Peace in Times of Shattered Romantic Idealism

13

Mrs and Mr Ganatra...I wrote on the card, kissing the envelope closed, my lips lingering on the 'Mr' a few seconds longer. I placed the cool champagne glass against my warm cheek, and turned up the volume of the song, '*When Lovers Become Strangers*', humming along to the lyrics:

You're looking at him across the room/
Wondering just how it all slipped away so soon/
You're looking to find some look in his eyes/
That will take you back to yesterday./
Don't remember the when or the where or why/
All you know is that something has changed inside/
And you can't bring it back no matter how you try /
You know it's over, you've got to say goodbye...

'Listen, just let it go,' Chandni quickly flipped tracks and pulled the card out of my fingers. She placed it in a corner away from the large pile of invites stacked on the dining room table, ready to be dispatched first thing Monday morning.

'I don't think you should invite him at all, Suchitra. Not after the way he behaved with you.'

Oh *puh-lease.* Why did they think I hadn't let it go? It's just...just that...*hmm*... well, shattered dreams or not, I was happy to make a sale. And besides the title of my exhibition

–'*The G-spot*[x]– was inspired by Pankaj, wasn't it? How could he not be there?

'Listen, the only reason I'm doing this is because...'

'Whatever the reason, best you don't!'

It had been over three long months since I had any contact with my muse. Three months of frenetic painting, week after week of doing nothing else but preparing for this exhibition. Day in and day out. My first solo show in four years, thirty-six works on display. I was nervous. The preview was less than a week away; the invitation cards had arrived late. It's a good thing I had already called up everybody to invite them on the phone but yet… And the fact that I was singing a few of my own songs at the opening was making me doubly edgy. My first music performance in over a decade. I was doing all that I could, exercising my vocal cords vigorously, having even quit the nicotine stick. It had taken a while for the rust to wear out but they were smooth and shiny now – ready to soar.

'You'll be fine, no worries. Nightingale will soon be your middle-name once again,' Sangita attempted a jangle of a rhyme, going off-key in her trademark boomerang. It made me wince but what the hell. Intention was everything. And I ***looovvved*** my girlfriends for all the good that was in them. None of this would have been possible otherwise.

'And, my darling, you're going to dazzle at the opening, so don't you worry,' Chandni beamed proudly, handing me a bottle of homemade jojoba almond face cream, insisting I start the beauty regimen right away.

'Erm...*now*? Can't it wait till tomorrow?'

'No. The best time to start anything is right now.' She smeared a large dollop on my cheek, announcing her plan to launch an exclusive range of cosmetics soon. It was apparently already a hit in her kitty party crowd, the only reason I had never condescended to try it so far.

'Good idea,' I said. 'But "*Chitty no kitty*", remember? Thank you very much.'

'No need to thank us, ya. Chill. We are your friends. Instead of this invite, just send Pankaj a thank-you note for curing you of your Aphallatosis. That is a favour he did to all of us.'

The bubbly was buzzing and fuzzing up our brain. We giggled and chirped and slurped some more.

Aphallatosis – a mental disorder resulting from lack of sex. A new word taught to me by Chandni in a desperate attempt to absolve herself of the Stanford University survey disaster. I had to concede she had been right on this one. The static in my head was gone forever.

'Let's Talk About Sex, Baby; Let's talk about you and me… Dang! Was my iPod skipping again? How had the song changed on its own accord? Was this some kind of trick just to get me thinking of that fateful day not so long ago, all over again?

That day when, after three short months of frenetic courting, Pankaj had simply deadpanned: 'I can't leave Amrita. Her shopping expenditure is cheaper than the alimony I would have to pay her.'

'But you said you love me?' I had squeezed the tears back into my eyeballs, clutching my thudding heart, ready to throw up. Just a few days ago we had talked about the names we would give our children. Gagan – which means sky, if it was a boy and …

'I never said that, Such. I'm sorry you understood it that way.'

How different his "Such" sounded now. No longer a lilting caress but a detached platitude. My stomach knotted. I buckled with the shock, holding on to the chair to stop myself from collapsing to the ground.

'What do you mean,"I'm sorry if I understood it that way"? Was everything we shared a lie, then?'

'No, it wasn't a lie. But I can't leave my wife. If you're okay with that we can continue to meet.'

If I am *okay* with that? What kind of a woman did he think I was? And Amrita – did he even care what her opinion on this was?

Pankaj's silence had said it all. I should have probed earlier. By the time I had discovered that what he'd meant by 'Amrita is moving out' was that she had merely shifted to another flat in the building they owned, it was too late. I was already smothered neck deep in the hurricane of lust – er, love.

'My marriage is fine,' Amrita had headlined in another interview in the *Bombay Times* where she had talked about her lavish extravagance in redesigning their home. And her pride at her husband Pankaj Ganatra's new-found praise of her Oniomania. She even used the word (which Pankaj had learnt from me, of course) this time, rather than 'shopping addiction'. They were hosting a house-warming soon. One to which I was obviously not invited.

After 72 hours of non-stop crying, bingeing on truckloads of pizza, banana chips and chocolate bars, chocolate pastry and some more dark chocolate, I plunged into painting with the rage of a fanatic.

Splashing it all on canvas, refusing Shrink's suggestion that I try a few more past-life regressions to heal myself.

'Who the hell let Madame Greedy in?' I could have killed Chandni.

'What else could I do, ya? I got scared. I thought you were having another…'

This was too much! Was this a trick? 'Another *what*?' When would my girlfriends *ever* learn about boundaries? 'I'm finally pulling myself together and you think I'm having another, *what*? I'm lucky I got this gallery booking because of an unexpected cancellation. I couldn't possibly let the opportunity pass.'

Amma hadn't been around this time to shoo Shrink away. So I was left to do the dirty work myself. So when Shrink refused to leave and continued to gaze at me with her pitying condescension, even having the gall to suggest that I should try expressing my emotions with the alphabet G this time – G for growth…G for goddess …G for blah blah blah, I dived for my cigarette lighter and clicked it dangerously close to Shrink's face over and over again, till she ran! The expression on her face had been priceless! Worth every penny of the hard-earned alimony I had paid her. G for Get lost, Shrink! I don't need you any more.

That had been my Eureka moment too. The title and theme of my exhibition had been born there and then.

So, naah, this was no trick. Just a reminder that we were rocking chicks!

'Clink clink. Bottoms up! I l*ooove* you, my girlies.'

'Let's Talk About Sex Baby/ Let's talk about you and me/ Let's talk about all the good things and the bad things that can be...' Sangita revved up the volume and before we knew it we were singing along at the top of our voices.

We laughed till our stomachs hurt. 'Shhsssh…Not so loud.'

It was past midnight. Kaveri was at her dad's. But Amma and Nana were in the next room. They were originally scheduled to return to Bangalore as soon as Kaveri's exams had ended yesterday, but had extended their stay by a week to be with me on my big day.

But my warning was too late – and all mothers are spies.

'Why are y'all laughing so loudly?' Amma charged out her room with her most pissed-off ever face. '*Aiyyo*, Chittappa. Why are you drinking wine again? I thought you had given up your bad habits.'

'It's not wine, Ma. It's champagne,' I offered her some.

Anger turned to disgust in the blink of an eye. Amma stared hard at the invitation card. '*G-spot*, aa? What sort of a title is that? Your last few exhibitions were titled *Faith* and *Pilgrimage* and all that – what is this "G-spot" now?'

'It's the last letter of the word "shopping",' Chandni giggled.

'It's a spot in the brain, Aunty – the good girl spot,' Sangita sent a beaming wink my way, attempting a quick cover-up for Chandni's regression into her Stanford university survey dumb dumb dumb days.

Considering Sangita had just returned from a meeting with the President of India on winning the HR award at a world business leaders' conference, (a fact that she had already mentioned about twenty times since the start of this evening) the way she was handling Amma was appalling.

'The G spot, Aunty. From where images of gods emerge,' Sangita took another large gulp of her bubbly. 'We are all good girls, you know.'

This pissed Amma off big time. 'What good girl? If you were

a good girl you would not be still seeing that schedule-caste fellow Mohan in spite of your mother's disapproval.' Amma flashed her world-famous scathing gaze: 'Don't think you girls can fool me. It's a good thing Chittu finally came to her senses. I had warned her too about that Gangotri chap…'

'Not Gangotri – Ganatra…' Amma was doing this deliberately, of course. She couldn't possibly be staring at his name written on the card and still be getting it all wrong. A trick! That's what it was.

'Gangotri or Ganatra what difference does it make? He's still a scoundrel.'

Schedule-caste, scoundrel, goat-lookalike, cunning chap… Amma's vocabulary was a class apart; in a league of its own. She was an unrecognized artist for sure. Maybe after this painting exhibition was behind me I would compile a book of Amma's put-downs for posterity. Call it *Dr Sulochana Krishnamoorthi's Handbook of Phobias, Insults and Oxymorons*'. Wow! What an idea. I had a plan. UGG! Rocking! I giggled

'Don't drink any more, ra Chittappa. Think about Kaveri. If you want to get married you better learn to start…'

'Start what, Amma? Can't you see how happy I am already starting to be? I'm enjoying my love affair with myself. Please let me do what I want to for once.'

'*Aiyyo*, why are you always contradicting everything, Chittu? *Chheh*!'

In spite of the long way I had come in healing – forgiving and letting go – there were still a few words that shot pellets into my brain, triggering off an uncontrollable response.

Chheh was one of them.

'Okay, in that case why don't you make a contribution to

my contradictions by going and making rasam rice for Kaveri instead of being such a party pooper, Amma?'

'Have you gone mad to ask me to go make rasam at this time in the night?' Tears sprung into Amma's eyes. 'All I asked is what G-spot means. Can't you give me a straightforward answer for anything? Why are you *always* overreacting? *Chheh*!'

Amma stormed away.

Chheh! *Chheh*!

Had I overreacted?

But it was my first celebration after months of back-breaking work.

Surely I deserved the break. How come Amma saw nothing but what she considered wrong?

'Chill, ya.'

My girlies and I tried to be as quiet as possible after Amma left. And though the party continued, the fun had fizzled out.

I could feel the first symptoms of the Boxer's Syndrome coming right back on...or was I really punch-drunk this time? *Hmm*...hard to tell.

Amma emerged almost an hour later again, a piece of paper clutched in her hands, her eyes red. Dang! *Now* what?

Amma walked right up and stood over me, compelling me to look at her. She cleared her throat and read aloud unflinchingly:

'The G-Spot: defined as a bean-shaped area of the vagina. Many women report that it is an erogenous zone which, when stimulated, can lead to strong sexual arousal, powerful orgasms and female ejaculation. It is also hypothesized that the G-Spot is an extension of the clitoris and that this is the cause of vaginal orgasms'

Shoot! I was dumbfounded!

'The internet is much better and far more informative than the dictionaries we used to have in our times. I wish I could have had this facility when I was doing research – I could have done so much more.'

'I'm sorry, Amma…'

'Why are you sorry, ra kanna?' *Sniff Sniff. Cry Cry.*

Dang!

'All I am telling you is to get rid of your bad habits – it's not good for Kaveri or for your health, that's all. But as an artist you have every right to express how you feel. I wish I had known about these things earlier myself. But in our times we women didn't even know what an orgasm was.'

Gasp! Gulp! Choke! Was I hearing this right? Had Amma just used the Big O Word? And that too so casually, without batting an eye? And was I was finally being acknowledged as an artist and a G-for-Grown-Up, to do as I please?

Yo mamma!

Spot on – *G-spot*-on!

'I think I'll go make some rasam for Kaveri. I have to do something now or I'll also go mad. I only hope that I have not caught the insomnia disease from you, Chittu.'

It was almost 2 a.m. for god's sake. But since Amma had kept her side of the pact we had made – of never asking me to marry Shekhar again –I had no choice but to stick to my side of the bargain – which was to allow her to feed Kaveri as much rasam rice or any other nutritionally-adequate foods that she considered appropriate for her granddaughter.

But wasn't there supposed to be a right time and place for everything?

Regardless of how much life had changed and how far we had come and all that?

'Amma, please that was just a joke. How can you make rasam now? Kaveri is not even here.'

Amma gazed at me the longest time, tears flowing down her cheeks, then abruptly turned her face away.

'So what if it's 2 a.m.? I'll send it to her at her daddy's house in the morning…'

'I'll help you, Aunty,' Chandni leapt out of the chair guiltily.

'No there is no need,' Amma shot back. 'Nanaa! *Naaana*,' she bellowed as she marched determinedly towards the kitchen.

'Please, Amma. There's no need to wake up Nana now.'

'What do you mean there is no need to wake up Nana? It is between me and him – you have no right to interfere.'

Ya right! Whatever!

'Why don't I show you some of my paintings, Amma? Then you'll understand why I called my exhibition the G-spot. There's nothing shameless in my work, I swear.' I put my arms around my mother's shoulders and lead her to the other room where the canvases were stacked up against the wall:

'See this one is called "Girlfriends",' I smiled. Amma stared hard.

GIRLFRIENDS

'The dark one is Sangita, no? Painting is okay – nothing great. I hope she's not planning to marry that schedule-caste fellow. I think I will speak to her mother about it before she does something stupid like you and ruins her life.'

'Amma, you promised me that you won't take off on my friends, remember? See this one – titled "Ganesha"...'

GANESHA

'How can Ganesha have breasts? I'm a teacher, ra kannappa. I agree I don't understand paintings much, but isn't there a limit to artistic liberty?'

We walked around the room, '*Aiyyo*, what is this one called now? Amma averted her eyes quickly.

'Erm, this one is called, it's called… *Hmm* …I wracked my brain and scratched my nose, 'It's called "*Good Girl*".'

GOOD GIRL:

'Good girl, aa? Why are you lying, ra kanna? That too, to your mother? If you are embarrassed about the title of your exhibition I suggest you change it. These things are nothing to be ashamed of…'

I was flabbergasted.

Really, Amma? No shit, Sherlock!

'Anyway, I have had enough. I don't want to see any more.' Amma stood there for many moments saying nothing and then suddenly wrapped her arms around me, tears welling in her eyes again.

I braced myself for another lecture on my shamelessness.

'I know I have never told you this before, but I am proud of you, ra kanna. All the best. Shine, ra chilaka. Goodnight.'

I stood there in stunned silence, my arms dangling awkwardly by my sides.

Wow. Cool Amma.

Cool Amma? Now what sort of an oxymoron was that?

A contradictory contribution or a true fiction?

Oh never mind.

I raised my arms and hugged my mother back tight, letting my tears flow into hers.

'I love you too, Amma. Goodnight.'

'What goodnight? Do you think I can go back to sleep now? You girls carry on with your party. I have definitely caught this insomnia disease from you, Chittu.'Nana! *Nanaa! Nanaaa!*

The ceiling shook and my teeth rattled.

'*Aiyyo!* That man snores like a buffalo! The day he hears me I can finally die in peace!'

Thank you

Farrukh Dhondy

Sorab Irani

Mahesh Dattani

Ram Gopal Varma

Karan Johar

Ken Ghosh

Nagesh Kukunoor